THE THREAT

by

Jonas Saul

PUBLISHED BY:

Imagine Press Inc.
Ebook ISBN: 978-1-927404-60-7
Paperback ISBN: 978-1-998047-88-8
Hardcover ISBN: 978-1-998047-87-1

The Threat
Copyright © 2011 by Jonas Saul

The Sarah Roberts Series

Dark Visions (One)
The Warning (Two)
The Crypt (Three)
The Hostage (Four)
The Victim (Five)
The Enigma (Six)
The Vigilante (Seven)
The Rogue (Eight)
Killing Sarah (Nine)
The Antagonist (Ten)
The Redeemed (Eleven)
The Haunted (Twelve)
The Unlucky (Thirteen)
The Abandoned (Fourteen)
The Cartel (Fifteen)
Losing Sarah (Sixteen)
The Pact (Seventeen)
The Terror (Eighteen)
The Chase (Nineteen)
The Betrayal (Twenty)
Sarah's Return (Twenty-One)
The Hunt (Twenty-Two)
The Delivery (Twenty-Three)
The Trap (Twenty-Four)
The Ultimatum (Twenty-Five)
The Depraved (Twenty-Six)
The Condemned (Twenty-Seven)
Payback (Twenty-Eight)
The Unknown (Twenty-Nine)
Wrath (Thirty)
The Damned (Thirty-One)
The Game (Thirty-Two)

The Decoy (Thirty-Three)
The Disappearance (Thirty-Four)
The Whole Truth (Thirty-Five)
Alex (Thirty-Six)
Parkman (Thirty-Seven)
Darwin (Thirty-Eight)
Aaron (Thirty-Nine)
Remains To Be Seen (Forty)

The Jake Wood Novels

The Immortal Gene (Book One)
The Immortal Target (Book Two)

Standalone Novels

'Til Death Do Us Part
The Drowning
The Woman in the Woods
The Threat
The Specter
The Mafia Trilogy
A Murder in Time
Frequency of the Dead

Co-Authored Novels

Collision Course (Written with Gary Ponzo)
There Will Be Blood (Written with Rania Stone)
The Soulless (Written with Rania Stone)

Short Story Collections

Twisted Fate (Tales of Horror)

The Threat

Twists of Fate (Tales of Hope)

Dedication

THIS NOVEL IS DEDICATED to all the officers who lay their lives on the line when they report for duty. This book is for police officers and platoon leaders like Sarah and Roman (personal friends and officers). Good people who put the force first and always do the right thing. I miss you and will always remember you. (You have a small mention in chapter thirteen)

The image of the Toronto Police Department at the G20 Summit and the speeches that officers make at universities, like the damaging one in January 2011, are only a small portion of the reality of hundreds of good officers across the nation who strive to serve and protect.

I dedicate this work of fiction to all the officers injured or dying at the hands of criminals in our society. The same community they swore to protect.

May they Rest in Peace.

During the writing of this novel, another officer was killed as he was dragged over three hundred meters by a minivan, which ended up on top of him.

This officer left behind a wife and two children.

May God bless Constable Garrett Styles. RIP

I also send out a tribute to *City Pulse 24* and *The Toronto Sun* for all of their years of tireless efforts to deliver the news to the people of Toronto and surrounding areas.

I miss you all and will always be in your debt.

Chapter 1

THE POURING RAIN SOAKED through Drake Bellamy's clothes as he studied the façade of the high-rise building on Victoria Park Avenue in Toronto, waiting for his meeting with the drug dealer. With ten minutes to wait, he shuffled from foot to foot, the rain cold against his skin.

The instructions he'd been given were simple. Enter the lobby, buzz 1408, and then ride the elevator to the fourteenth floor. Once he was at the apartment door, he was to knock twice, pause, and then three more times. Simple, but strangely covert, too. Why all the hiding and sneaking around? It was only a little weed.

He stepped from the sidewalk and sauntered across the wet grass. It would be all over soon. He had to get upstairs, meet some guy named Charles, pay him a hundred bucks for a small quantity of medical weed, and get the hell out. There was nothing to it.

"Who am I kidding?" he asked himself. "I could get busted for this."

Drake had no choice in the matter. His mother had cancer and was in constant pain. It was a huge fight with the Canadian bureaucracy to get medical marijuana. She was still months away from obtaining her license, so his father had given him this contact over the phone.

Everything would be fine, he assured himself. All the same, this really sucked. If he was going to break the law, at least he was doing it for the right reasons.

A woman with two small children entered the apartment building's main door as Drake stepped up. He grabbed the handle and held the door for her. She walked past him without a glance his way, pulling her children along after her. She lifted her raincoat's hood and entered the downpour, becoming a blur of yellow moments later. Her children repeatedly protested the rain by whining about their mother's name.

Once through the lobby doors, he realized just how wet he was as the air conditioners worked to cause every goosebump on his body to rise to the surface of his skin. He found the doorbell panel, and with his index finger, he scanned the list of names and apartment numbers, stopping at 1408.

Keeley, Anne.

He took one last look around before committing himself to the illegal drug purchase. No one was in the lobby. Outside, only the woman and her two kids walked the sidewalk he'd been on minutes before. Several vehicles and a city bus passed by on the street. No one paid him any attention, his purpose undetected.

What could go wrong?

He pressed the buzzer. A low metallic sound emitted from the circular speaker embedded in the middle of the large console.

He waited, a clock ticking in his head. Maybe no one was home. Maybe they forgot he was coming.

He glanced over his shoulder. The mid-afternoon timeframe had seemed perfect. Most people would be at work. Anyone home in this building wouldn't want to brave the heavy rain.

"Hello?"

He was still leaning forward when the metallic voice startled him. He jumped and lost his balance just enough to bump into the row of buttons, creating a dreadful cacophony of noise that sounded like a dying synthesizer.

"Um, yeah, hello," he said, attempting to sound like he had it together.

"Come on up—"

The man's voice was drowned out by the five or six other voices competing for a spot from all the buzzers he'd accidentally pushed.

The access door clicked. He opened it and headed for the elevators.

Now, he felt like a criminal. It was as though he was going upstairs to visit a prostitute for an hour, and the police were waiting for him. The point of no return had come and gone. He had chosen to do this for his mother. If his dad hadn't supplied the address, he would have had no idea where to buy this kind of thing.

Everything's going to be fine.

No one was getting arrested today. If he did, he would

opt for trial by jury—if that was possible. Once the jury heard he did it to ease the pain of his sick mother, a woman who didn't have long to live, he'd be sent home with a warning. *And* he was a first-time offender.

Everything's going to be fine.

Waiting for the elevators to come from the floors above, he heard a couple of stragglers on the intercom asking who was there. The door clicked again behind him. Then, someone swore over the intercom.

"I'm coming for you, mutherfucka …"

Drake turned back to the elevator. "Come on, come on," he whispered under his breath.

A look each way down the hall of the first floor revealed empty carpeted hallways.

Ding.

The elevator doors opened slowly. He made to jump on but had to step back as two huge black men were coming off.

"What the fuck?" the tall one said. "Give us some room, white boy."

"Sorry," Drake said. He ambled past them and onto the elevator. He pushed fourteen and only had to wait a few seconds before the doors began to shut. Both black men had turned and stared holes into him as the doors closed.

The tallest one blew out of his lips disrespectfully, telling Drake in one breath that he wasn't worth it.

The doors closed. Relative safety. He took a deep breath and leaned on the wall. What was this place? Why's everyone so angry? Is it a black building or something, and being white would be a problem?

He felt even colder as his shirt and light jacket were glued to his skin like a wet paste. A shiver ran through him, shaking his shoulders.

Okay, get it together. This is almost over.

The elevator slowed and stopped at fourteen. The doors opened, and he stepped into the hallway. Instantly, he was assailed with a food smell. Someone was cooking Indian food very close to the elevators. Scents of turmeric and other spices congested the air. It made him think someone had cooked the hell out of a curry dish and decided to feed the fourteenth floor its last meal.

He walked to the left only to realize within a couple of doors that he was going the wrong way. After passing the elevators again, the smell intensified once more. He brought his sleeve up to breathe through it and only succeeded in wetting his mouth and nose.

"Shit."

Apartment 1408 came up on his right. In front of the door, he adjusted his jacket and knocked. One more look up and down the empty hallway to calm his nerves. After about twenty seconds, he knocked again. Why were they taking so long? He had buzzed up first. They knew he was coming.

The code. *The fucking code.* He stomped his foot.

"Shit."

This time, he knocked twice and paused, then knocked three times.

The door was opened instantly. So fast that Drake stepped back, hands clenched as if he would have to defend himself.

A bald man smiled back at him.

So it wasn't a black building, after all.

"Come in, come in. You look wet. Lotta rain, eh?"

The man stepped back, gestured with his arm to enter,

and Drake walked into the apartment.

"Here, let me take your coat."

Drake eased out of the jacket and handed it to the bald guy who looked to be in his early forties.

"I'll hang it on the closet doorknob here."

The man seemed at least ten years older than Drake. A snake tattoo appeared from under his collared shirt and wrapped around his left ear, the forked tongue of the asp aimed toward the ear canal.

"Come into the dining room, where we'll discuss terms."

Drake hadn't said a word yet. The truth was, he didn't know what to say. This was his first time, and as first times go, he was as nervous as a pilot with flashing lights on his panel, the cabin pressure dropping, and a flap not working.

He examined everything as they passed through the apartment's kitchen and headed toward the dining room. The counters had limited space, but every bit of it was used up with small appliances. The dishes sat unwashed in the sink. Drake took a quick look to see the kind of food these people ate as there was an odor in the apartment he couldn't quite identify.

The dining room was another story. The table was littered with dishes. Leftover parts of a turkey or a large chicken sat on a cutting board in the center of the table.

"You guys must've just eaten," Drake said. "I hope I didn't come at a bad time."

"That's from last night. Been busy taking care of something else. We'll clean up after you're gone. Have a seat here."

Drake couldn't place the guy's European accent. Central Europe somewhere, like Romania or Bulgaria. Possibly

Hungarian.

He sat at the head of the table in front of a plate with gristle, a couple of bones, and leftover scraps.

"Move it aside." His host piled a couple of plates on the side. "As I said, cleanup is later." The man stood back and crossed his arms. The collar shirt he wore had the sleeves half rolled up. When he crossed them, the sleeves pulled back enough to reveal a red splotch on the bottom of his forearm that resembled blood.

"You may have cut yourself," Drake said, pointing at the arm with the mark.

The bald guy uncrossed his arms and looked. "That's nothing." He ran a finger through the mark and placed the finger on his tongue. "Cranberry sauce." He recrossed his arms and looked at Drake. "Tell me what you have come here for?"

The guy knew why he was there. It had all been a setup. Drake had no idea where his dad got the information, and he hadn't asked. He was just supposed to get a hundred bucks out of a bank machine, come to this apartment, buy some medical weed, and leave. Quick and simple.

"Let me make it easier," Baldy said. "Are you here for something specific?"

"Yes."

"Look, I can't offer you anything unless you ask for it. Or ..." the bald guy tilted his head to the side. "Are you a cop?"

"No, no." Drake raised his hands in defense. "I came to buy drugs. I mean, medical weed. It's for my mother. She has cancer."

There, he said it. All blurted out at once, without even

checking if the bald guy was a cop first. He'd committed himself now. No going back.

To break the law and be convicted, you need to establish two things: one, the intent, and two, the act of breaking the law. Drake was pretty sure the intent part was just handled. The act was coming.

The bald guy smiled. "This your first time?"

"Yeah." Drake averted his eyes. He fumbled with the dish in front of him and moved the utensils aside so he could place his elbows on the table. He knew he looked nervous but couldn't do anything about it.

"It's okay. I get first-timers often. I have everything in the other room. Give me a few minutes to get it, and I'll be right back."

The bald guy walked away with a smug look, leaving Drake to sit alone in the dining room with a table full of dirty dishes. Why the smug look, though? It was like he had won something, some small victory. He had Drake right where he wanted him. He was the master in charge, and Drake was the puppet. Something about it made Drake want to get up from the table and run from the apartment.

If his stomach *could* be any more upset, dealing with the bald guy just added to it.

Why didn't Snake Head ask about quantity? How much was he getting? Or did his father already deal with that? He had only brought the hundred bucks his father told him to get for the deal. He had even left his wallet at home in case he got jumped—no ID. This wasn't his first time buying drugs —it was his first time coming to this part of Toronto and the first time making a deal with a criminal.

Maybe he'd been watching too much TV.

Deals like this happen all over the place all day long. You only hear about deals gone bad and shootings when territorial disputes exist or someone's trying to rip off another dealer. Simple deals like this one not only happened often, but it was exactly why a dealer remained in business in the first place. To make steady money.

Drake looked back into the kitchen. He was close enough to the stove to see the time. It was 2:12 p.m. How long was this going to take?

To pass the time, he counted the dishes. Three people ate there last night. They ate well, by the looks of it.

He fumbled his fingers, tapped his feet, and looked out the window through the sheer curtains. He turned back to the stove. 2:14 p.m.

Sirens sent up a shrill wail from somewhere in the distance. It didn't surprise him. In this neighborhood, he was sure they would always hear sirens.

I'd hate to be the guy they're looking for.

He thought back to the one time he had trouble with the law. It was an old girlfriend issue in high school. They'd planned on eloping. Taking off, getting married, and living in her country. Four months before they were to leave, his girlfriend had disappeared. Police investigated it. He was questioned relentlessly.

There had been an incident. A fight, a struggle of some kind, and Drake had been knocked out. When he woke, Monika was gone. Months later, she was located alive in Budapest, and the case was filed as closed. He remembered the intense hours of grilling by the cops. They had said they didn't believe him, that he was lying and knew where she was. They asked about the scuffle. Why was he found unconscious? But most of that evening was blocked for Drake. He could only remember that they had gone to the park by the lake to talk. To discuss their plans to elope. He never saw her or heard from her again. That was twelve years ago when he was eighteen, and she was seventeen.

Police sirens have always messed him up since those days as if they were coming for him. As a police car approached, he would say to his friends, "There's my ride."

The clock on the stove read 2:18 p.m.

What the hell? Where is he?

The distant sirens had gotten much closer. It sounded like they were pulling up outside. Drake got up and walked to the dining room window. Without going onto the balcony, he saw four Toronto Police cruisers speeding through the rain and slowing to take the turn into the access for the building he was in.

From where he stood, the four cruisers disappeared from view under the balcony ledge. He stepped back from the window, wondering who would garner such a response and what they might have done.

Nagging doubt made him consider they were there for him, but he knew it couldn't be as his dad had set up the meeting. The guy knew what Drake was here for, and the deal was about to be completed at any second.

No way there was a problem.

He stepped around the table and entered the kitchen.

2:22 p.m.

He had sat for over ten minutes. This was taking far too long. If the guy were on the phone or otherwise distracted, Drake would be pissed. Maybe the bald fucker was smoking up first.

His hands shook with a nervous twitch.

He had come here to make a deal and stated as such. His part was over. He wanted to leave as soon as possible, walk the six blocks to the other side of the mall, and drive back to Mississauga, where he would feel more comfortable in his own apartment.

He passed through the kitchen and stood by the main apartment door.

After a moment, he called out. "Hello?"

No one answered.

Did the guy have to take a shit or something?

He moved into the living room. A unique set of couches had leopard skin blankets tossed across them. The shag carpet looked like it was from the seventies. A widescreen TV sat on the wall like a painting.

"Hello? You still around?"

No answer.

"I need to get going. Can we speed this up?"

His shirt had almost dried, but the remaining dampness stuck to his skin, making him shiver. He wondered if he should put on his jacket as it wouldn't have completely dried yet either.

More sirens pulled up out front. Now, he was getting freaked out. Something was wrong. Drake fought the urge just to walk away and get out of there.

Maybe the cops were coming to bust the bald guy? Maybe after all the deals he'd done, someone ratted him out? That would be perfect. On the one day, the one deal Drake needed, the bald guy gets busted. Wouldn't that be great fucking timing?

"Hello. Anybody home?"

The bedroom door sat ajar. He walked past the couch and headed for the bedroom door.

He placed his mouth near the crack in the door. "Hello?"

That nasty smell lingering near the kitchen was stronger here. It emitted from the bedroom, filling his nostrils.

"You all right in there?"

After still getting no response, he opened the door slowly.

Dizziness made him grab for the doorframe as his stomach clenched. He spun around and ran for the bathroom door that stood open.

He didn't make it.

Vomit spewed forth and hit the wall beside the bathroom. His breakfast gone, he turned back and stumbled to the bedroom door again, gasping and spitting out the last of the bile taste in his mouth.

It had to be a joke. There was no way this was possible. He needed to confirm it. If it was real, therapy was right around the next corner. If it was set up for whatever reason, he could leave, knowing there are many sick people in the world.

At the bedroom door, he glanced inside. Everything seemed real enough. This was no stage prop. He'd never smelled anything like it before.

A woman lay naked on the bed. She had been cut open as if someone had performed a vivisection. Her innards were pulled out and scattered around the loose skin of her abdomen. Blood had seeped from her vaginal area, indicating to Drake that she was alive when that area was abused. There were bruises on her face and neck. Deep purple and red marks surrounded her nipples. In the few seconds Drake stared at the body on the bed, he could tell she had been beaten, choked, raped, and then stabbed and cut open, and finally, killed.

Who could do such a thing? Who would want to?

A deep sadness darkened his consciousness. He felt utterly sick. His legs were weak, and his hands trembled against the door frame. How could a human being do this to another?

He needed to leave. He had to get out of this apartment. It was a murder scene, and he had nothing to do with it.

He ran to the front door to grab his jacket and leave but stopped. What about his vomit? He had to clean that up first. Although, wouldn't that look suspicious? If they ever found out he'd been in the apartment and then he'd taken measures to conceal that fact, he'd look even more guilty. It would take years to sort it out.

No one had samples of his DNA. No one had his fingerprints anywhere. There was no way they could tie him to this apartment, let alone the building. This part of Scarborough was new to him. No one would recognize him or know him. The best thing to do was get the fuck out.

He reached for the door handle but stopped when he heard shuffling on the other side.

He edged close to the door to look through the peephole.

Four Toronto police officers stood on the other side of the door. One was motioning to someone down the hall to continue forward. Then he pointed at the apartment door of 1408.

Behind which stood Drake Bellamy and a dead female occupant.

He needed to leave. He'd done nothing wrong. The

police officer's job wasn't to play the judge and jury. They would arrest him and let the courts figure it out. He couldn't spend the next year in jail waiting for that to happen. It wasn't fair. He had done nothing wrong.

Fuck it. I'm outta here.

Drake turned from the door, grabbed his jacket, and ran for the balcony. Behind him, someone knocked so hard it sounded like they were using a hammer. Then a cop yelled, "Toronto Police, open up!"

Drake moved the curtains aside and tried to unlock the balcony door. His fingers were wet from the jacket. He couldn't maintain a solid grip on the lock. He tossed his jacket on the nearest couch, wiped his fingers on one of the leopard blankets, and yanked on the lock again.

It snapped open as the police pounded on the door incessantly behind him.

Drake slid the door aside quietly and then the screen door. A table and two chairs were on the balcony. He moved the table closer to the retaining wall, separating the neighbor's balcony from the one he was on.

A loud bang emanated from inside the apartment. The police were attempting to break the door down.

Certain only seconds separated him from being caught in the apartment with a dead body, Drake got up on the table and looked around the edge to the other balcony. Being careful not to look down the fourteen floors to the ground, he got a full view of the mountain bike and golf clubs the neighboring tenant stored on their balcony.

He heard another bang from inside the apartment behind him. The rain poured down past his shoulders. He put his foot on the railing and tested it for good measure. With only seconds left, Drake lifted off the table and stepped onto the wet ledge of the balcony, over one-hundred-forty feet above the ground, his hands gripping the concrete partition as best he could.

Then he looked down.

It was unavoidable. His balance wavered as his hands struggled for purchase.

Fourteen floors up, he could count eight cruisers parked in front of the building.

The second he hesitated, he saw a cop looking up at him. The cop raised his arm and pointed. Other people looked up, too.

His feet slipped on the wet railing.

He spun toward the other balcony and reached for the far side. His hand found a piece of concrete jutting out, as luck would have it. It gave him something to hold on to as leverage. His right foot came around and plunked down on the neighbor's railing at the exact moment his left foot slid off the other. Without delay, he hopped down onto the floor of the neighbor's balcony, lost his balance, and fell to his side.

A huge sigh escaped him as he realized he had almost met the Grim Reaper.

More noises could be heard from the other apartment.

They had to be inside now.

How was he going to get out? The cops would be watching every door in the hallway. A cop had seen him jump onto this balcony. He would radio up to his fellow officers what he'd seen.

It was over. He had tried to run, but they caught him.

"Damn," he said as he slammed a fist into his palm. "I

forgot my fucking jacket on the couch back there."

He grabbed the balcony door to see if it was locked. It slid open with ease. Under normal circumstances, he would be happy with this lucky break, but he was in their trap as sure as being mired in quicksand.

Unless …

He ran through the apartment, heading for where he thought the bedroom was, with no regard for the fact that someone could be home. Whether someone was home mattered little if his plan didn't succeed. Yet the fact that the apartment was empty affirmed that his chances of getting out were increasing.

In the bedroom, he located the closet, grabbed two random T-shirts, changed into one on top of the other, tossed his damp shirt on the floor, and ran back into the living room. He reached the apartment door and looked through its peephole to the hallway. A cop ran by the door. Then another. They had the floor covered. This would take brains, courage, and a ton of luck.

He turned from the door and screamed at the empty living room. "What the fuck are you doing in my apartment? Get outta here. How did you get in?"

With his right hand, he smacked his face hard enough to leave red marks.

"Hey, what the—"

He smacked himself again. Then grabbed the collar of the T-shirt and ripped it an inch.

"I'm calling the police if you don't leave right now," he yelled at the empty apartment.

Drake bodychecked the door hard. Then he unlocked it and opened it.

Three Toronto police officers stood staring at him. One of them had his hand up with a container of pepper spray in it. The other two had their hands on the butts of their guns.

"Where did you guys come from?" he shouted. "How'd you get here so fast?" Drake gasped breaths in and out as if he'd just run a marathon. If only they knew it was his nerves and heart rate causing him to nearly collapse. "Don't just stand there. Do something. Some guy jumped onto my balcony from that apartment," Drake pointed in the direction of the Snake Head drug dealer's place, "and accosted me in my own home."

Two of the officers reacted. They brushed past Drake and into the apartment behind him. He stepped aside and moved down the hall a few feet, holding his face where he'd been slapped.

"Don't get too far," the remaining cop said. "We're gonna need to talk to you."

Drake had made it ten feet away. He was only five feet from the door to the stairwell.

"I'll wait over here. I don't want to be too close when that thug comes out."

Someone yelled from inside the apartment.

They'd found his wet shirt on the floor in the bedroom.

The ruse was up.

Drake bolted for the stairwell. By the time he got through the door and was down the first flight of steps, he heard heavy footfalls directly behind him.

They were close and moving in fast. He had to think of something. The trap had not been completely sprung yet.

On the twelfth floor, he opened the door to the hall and turned to close it. Drake bolted along the corridor as fast as his weak legs would carry him, but it was useless. He needed to get to the other end before a cop could enter the door behind him, which wouldn't happen.

While running the corridor length, he banged on the apartment doors. He knocked on every door he passed and yelled one word repeatedly.

"Fire!"

Then, with deft precision, he yanked down the red handle on a fire alarm unit as he passed it. The entire building went live with the sound of the shrill scream of the alarm.

Doors opened behind him. He looked over his shoulder to see one of those doors was to the stairwell. Numerous cops barreled through. One of them lifted his arm and yelled for Drake to stop.

Other doors opened between them. Five or six people randomly entered the twelfth-floor hallway, standing between the cops and Drake. He saw all this as he neared the entrance to the far stairwell. He was sure the cops were yelling things like *freeze* and *get outta the way*, but no one would be able to hear them as the fire alarm was so loud.

Drake hit the stairwell door at the other end of the hallway and raced down the stairs to the floors below. Other people were entering the stairwell ahead of him, alerted by the alarm and not wanting to risk the elevator. He mixed in with the descending crowd. By the time he got to the sixth floor, he had removed the torn T-shirt and tossed it onto the floor. Its purpose was served.

Now dressed in an orange Dead Head T-shirt, he tousled his hair and continued downward. Adrenaline pumped through his veins like it had been injected straight from a can of Red Bull.

He had lost the hundred bucks as that was in his jacket pocket back in the drug dealer's living room. He had lost his jacket and his cookies in the same apartment. He had even left his fingerprints on the plate and utensils he'd touched at the dining room table. The only thing he still had were his car keys. Luckily, those were things he always placed in his jeans pocket.

As he passed the third floor surrounded by running tenants, he wondered if he had also lost his sanity. Was he crazy? Why *was* he running? He'd done nothing wrong. By that rationale, there were zero reasons to run.

Yet he ran.

He didn't even get to buy the drugs, thereby committing no act of breaking the law. He was as innocent as they come.

Yet he ran.

The first floor came up quickly. He'd have to deal with the unusual semantics of his situation another time. The door to the first floor was wide open, but most people continued down the stairs, racing right by the first-floor door.

When Drake turned the corner, he saw why.

A large red exit sign hung over the door to the outside, where the people ahead of him were filing out. It was slow going as everyone seemed to clump together at the door.

He was almost free.

Through the opening, it looked like the rain had stopped. People were gathering in groups. Neighbors, friends, and relatives stood talking to one another, asking if the others knew anything.

The moment Drake got to the door, his heart jolted. Two Toronto cops were standing on either side, monitoring the faces of the people exiting the building.

Back into his acting mode, he turned his face into a mask of discontent, appearing miffed at the intrusion of a fire alarm. He even yawned as he stumbled out the door. As a last-minute thought, he turned to the guy behind him and said, "Working the night shift sucks when you get these alarms in the middle of the day like this."

Both cops were in earshot. He knew they heard him. As he passed them, they waved him on.

Drake was out.

They weren't looking for a thirty-year-old in an orange Dead Head T-shirt who was yawning and complaining about being woken up. They were looking for a guy who was running ragged, with a ripped neckline on his T-shirt, and who had wet hair.

Drake walked through the throng of people on the lawn, up to the sidewalk, and across Victoria Park Avenue. On the way to his car, his legs weakened, the adrenaline wearing off. He turned around several times, but no one followed him.

He'd gotten away clean.

Ten minutes later, he saw his car sitting right where he'd left it. Ensconced in the front seat, his hands shook too much to get the key in. Drake sat there and tilted his head back to lean it on the headrest, trying to get his breathing under control.

Tears came. He wept for what he had seen for the nameless girl that had been so brutally killed. He cried for the people who could've done such a thing. How was this possible? Why set *him* up? How was his father involved? Nothing added up, and everything felt wrong on so many levels.

Pictures of the woman's naked corpse assailed his mind

over and over, causing him to feel sick again.

He needed to get home to feel safe. He needed out of here, but could he drive? Was he capable of operating a motor vehicle?

Drake tried the key again, and it went in without a problem. He turned the car on, dropped it into gear, and looked over his shoulder.

The bald guy from the apartment stood a hundred feet away, smiling, watching him.

Drake froze. His Pontiac idled, his foot on the brake, hand on the steering wheel.

The bald guy stood beside a large blue pickup truck about thirty meters back. Their eyes locked for what felt like minutes but were mere seconds.

Then Snake Head did something that made Drake almost lose it completely.

He reached his midsection and jerked his hand up and down, indicating the vivisection wound on the girl in the apartment. With his left hand, he pointed at Drake to indicate he was next. Then he ran a hand across his neck in the international symbol of cutting one's throat.

Drake pulled away. It was the only response he had. The only thing he could do. It was obvious the bald guy meant him harm. Somehow, he had been pegged for this.

What the bald guy probably hadn't accounted for was that Drake would make it out of that building.

The bald guy also missed the point that Drake would now be a wanted man.

Drake wasn't the fighting type. He didn't want this, nor did he ask for it. But fear had a way of changing a man. The fear of being taken by the police caused him to act in ways he never thought he would.

The fear of threats caused anger to rise in him.

Staring at the bald guy as he mocked the girl's death in the apartment and then slit his throat with his finger to indicate to Drake what was coming caused violence to stir in Drake that he never thought possible.

At that moment, he realized he would probably have to kill the bald guy or be killed by him, yet he still had no idea why it was happening.

Chapter 2

SEVERAL POLICE CRUISERS PASSED Drake on the Gardiner Expressway as he drove to his apartment, but none paid him any attention. Exhausted from the ordeal, he plopped on his couch to think about what had happened.

What was he going to do? He had no idea who the bald guy was or why he tried to set him up. And why was that girl murdered? What could she have done to deserve that kind of violence?

The big question was how long it would take the police to catch up with him. Drake would be an easy guy to find. He had a health card, a debit card, and a Visa. He paid rent, worked as a forklift operator at a loading dock in Etobicoke, and paid his taxes on time. Any government computer could be summoned to give up everything from his middle name and date of birth to his last bowel movement.

He saw no future in hiding and no end in running, either.

Who could live off the grid nowadays?

He turned to his side and lay down on the couch. It was mid-afternoon. It would be right now if there were ever a time to stop and think. After today, he would be like the guy in that movie, *The Fugitive*, running from the police while attempting to solve the murder before they caught up to him.

And what about his father? Why would he send him to meet Charles Manson's brother? Didn't he check the name and address before randomly delivering his son up shit creek?

Drake closed his eyes and monitored his breathing. Besides the shakes that were wearing off, he was coming back around, the rush of the past few hours ebbing.

When he opened his eyes, the apartment had grown dark. He looked around, assuming that someone had turned off the lights. No one was in the apartment. The drapes were open, and the street lights outside were lit.

He must've fallen asleep. After standing and a quick stretch to awaken his muscles, he walked into the kitchen and saw that it was almost eleven in the evening.

"I slept for over five hours," he whispered to himself.

So much could have happened in that time. He turned to the fridge and began to prepare something to eat. Once a sandwich was made in under a minute, he devoured it in four large bites.

After eleven in the evening, he sat down in front of the TV to check in on the local news. He turned to *City Pulse 24*, the all-news channel.

His face was displayed on the screen. A police sketch artist had done a mock-up of all the witnesses. The reporter was at the scene of a brutal murder in an apartment building in the 700 block of Victoria Park Avenue. A woman had been beaten, raped, and stabbed to death.

"Homicide detectives are looking for this man. He was witnessed entering the building by a woman with her two children. The woman said he appeared to be quite rude."

The screen changed to film the legs of two men.

"These two men claim the suspect wanted to fight them in the building lobby as they came off the elevator."

"Can you tell us anything else?" the reporter asked.

"Yeah, man, this dude was crazy. We be walking off the elevator, minding our own bizness, and he be all up in our face and asking us what our problem was. My cuz and I don't understand white dudes coming up on our turf and saying sh —(beep) like that."

"Police are getting close to identifying this man."

Drake's picture was back on the screen.

"This man is considered armed and extremely dangerous. If you see this man, do not approach him. Call the Toronto Police at ..."

He turned off the TV. Lies, all lies. Those guys called *him* on. The woman with the kids was rude to *him*. He didn't kill anyone, yet the police were looking for him for murder.

This wasn't a dream as much as a nightmare. There is no way all this could be happening.

He reached the end of the couch and grabbed the phone, his hand shaking. After pressing the number four and holding it down, the phone speed-dialed his parents' place.

Six rings and voicemail picked up.

He knew his parents would be asleep by this hour, but he still wanted to talk to his dad. He needed answers, and he needed them right away.

There was nowhere to turn, nowhere to run. He was wanted for murder, which translated to his life was over.

A light flashed across the ceiling of his apartment. Drake sank into the couch as if he could disappear through the cushion. He studied the stucco roof, waiting to see it again.

Nothing.

The only window was the living room window. He was on the second floor of Maplewood Towers. It was conceivable that a car's headlights could have crossed the window and bounced off his ceiling.

Only, he'd never seen that before.

Instead of checking the window and the surrounding area outside, Drake got up and checked the apartment door to see if he'd locked it when he got home earlier that afternoon.

The door was bolted.

He turned into the kitchen, retrieved a steak knife from the set on his counter, and made his way slowly to the edge of the curtains on the right side of the window. The apartment was dead quiet. No sound was emitted from the surrounding apartments, either. Only a random car or two would pass below this time of night.

Unless the police had found him. Maybe they were preparing to storm the building and take him by surprise.

He edged the curtains away from the wall. From his vantage point, he saw nothing untoward. There was no movement except for one vehicle driving west on Bloor Street. He watched it go until it was lost from view.

His thinking became clearer. A part of him wondered if he was a military man in a past life. How could he fall into the role of a fugitive so easily? Earlier that day, back in the apartment next to 1408, putting on the two T-shirts as he did had surprised him as if he knew the plan and how to execute it. But he hadn't. At the time, it had struck him as a good idea.

He let the curtain fall from his hand as nothing else moved outside. Maybe he was being paranoid—although with good reason.

He stepped in front of the glass and looked through from the center area where the light would've come in. There was something on the window near the left-hand corner. He bent to have a look, moving the curtain on that side out of the way.

A word was written on the glass.

When he got the curtain completely out of the way, he saw it for what it was.

Got You.

He eased back. *Got who?* Who could've written that? When did they write it? When he was asleep?

He leaned in closer to examine the message again. It was written in the window's condensation—on the *inside* of the window.

That meant either he wrote it in his sleep, or someone else had been in the apartment.

Or that someone was still there.

Drake turned from the window, stood to his full height, and lifted the steak knife.

"Hello?" he asked out loud.

Not again, he thought. *I just did this.*

"Anyone there?"

He received no response. The apartment was dark except for the dim light from the streetlights and parking lot lights close to his apartment.

He grabbed his wallet and cell phone, dropped the steak knife on the end table by the couch, and got to the apartment door without incident. The peephole on the door looked out onto an empty hallway.

He opened the door, stepped out into the lighted hall, and locked the apartment door behind him. He looked both ways and chose the closest stairwell. It would only take one flight of stairs, and then he'd be outside and in his car.

With no destination in mind, he headed down the corridor with an urgency he felt in his bones. Someone had been in his apartment. Probably while he slept. Whoever these people were, they were excellent lock pickers because the bolt on the door had remained secure. If their goal was to kill or attack him, why not do something about it when he was asleep? Why taunt him?

"What the fuck is going on?" he asked the empty corridor.

Down the stairs and outside into the cool June evening was easy. It was the walk through the parking lot that tore at his ability to remain calm, knowing that losing it now would not be cool.

He turned to the right and saw the bald guy's pickup truck. It was parked in the corner of the lot. He squinted but couldn't discern anyone behind the wheel.

Drake slowed and turned to look up at his balcony. No lights were evident behind the dark windows. Should he go back up to the apartment? He shook his head—this wasn't the time for a confrontation. He needed to figure things out first. Maybe the light he'd seen on the ceiling was a flashlight beam from the bedroom where the bald guy had been hiding. Perhaps he'd finished what he was doing in there and made to leave but got caught by surprise as he saw Drake sitting up on the couch, awake.

No, the intruder would've heard the television.

Six steps from his Pontiac, Drake realized that he should have checked the whole apartment before leaving. What if they planted something? What had happened earlier in Scarborough wasn't random. This guy and whoever else was involved wanted to set up Drake.

He took another glance at the pickup. Was that even the bald guy's truck?

A car passed on Bloor Street. Drake made it to his car. He inserted the key, unlocked the door, and opened it.

A loud metallic sound made him jump. Hairs rose all over his body as he tried to ascertain what caused the noise.

Then, another one made him jump again.

A flash of light caught his eye. He looked to the left and saw the bald guy standing there, his right arm raised and pointed at Drake.

A third metal clanging sound came after the bald guy's extended arm emitted a short burst of light.

I'm being shot at.

In that second of realization, Drake glanced at his car and saw three small bullet-sized holes in the door.

Holy shit.

He ripped open the door, dove in, jammed the key into the ignition, and cranked the engine. It started instantly.

His heart rate beating off the charts, Drake dropped it into gear and dared a peek above the dashboard as far as he could to see where he was going. Two more metallic bangs resounded in the relative quiet of the neighborhood.

By the time Drake had fully turned the car around,

squealed to the parking lot exit, and got as far away from the bald guy as he could, one more shot from the guy's gun shattered Drake's back window.

He screamed as the glass cascaded in tiny pieces throughout the interior.

It was almost midnight. No cars were passing Maplewood Towers when Drake hit the gas in a frenzy and almost lost control of the wheel as he turned onto Bloor.

He hit the curb, lifted up onto the grass, and turned back into the road, finally correcting the steering and racing straight away from his building like he had a broken cage of weasels scurrying around inside the car.

Chapter 3

He knew what would happen next. The police would be called to Maplewood Towers because of the gunfire. Someone in his building would recognize his picture. Within an hour of the authorities showing up at his building, they would have a name for the face. They would also have his apartment and whatever else the bald guy had done to further his aim—whatever madness that aim may be.

He had to stop it but couldn't come up with a solution. Maybe he could call a lawyer and explain everything. Then, together, they could meet with the police and tell them his side of the events. He'd even take a polygraph. But wouldn't that look like an admittance of guilt to lawyer up?

It was after midnight. He had nowhere to go and a busted-out back window. He could get pulled over for that alone, and then everything would blow up in his face.

He'd just been shot at. Maybe that was something? At

least he could prove it with the holes in his car.

It occurred to him that he needed to get to his dad before the police did. Once they realized who he was, they'd know where to find his parents. He couldn't stay with them—too risky—but he could go and wake his father to get some answers. Perhaps a change of clothes, a shower, and a shave. Then he'd change vehicles.

He drove the speed limit and, at times, under it. The empty side streets and less-traveled roads were safer. One reason was to hide from the authorities so he wouldn't get pulled over. The other was to avoid being followed by that bald fucker.

He checked his mirrors too many times and drove carefully but continued without interruption through the dark Toronto night.

He was fifteen minutes from his parents' house on Hunter Street in the Jones and Pape area of the Danforth when he couldn't shake the image of the snake tattoo on the side of the head of the bald guy. Who was he? What did he want? Was Drake a random pick to terrorize? Did the idiot do this often so he could murder people and get someone else arrested for his crime?

Even if someone hired Snake Head to go after Drake, who could that be? Drake didn't have any enemies that he knew of. Thinking back on his life, there might be a few schoolmates he bugged, but that was child's play. He was swarmed once in a mall and punched in the face, but they were the aggressors, and that was many years ago. Nothing in his life was ever serious enough for *murder*.

Maybe the girl's identity in apartment 1408 could shed some light on what was happening.

He could use a camera. Next time, he would take a picture of the bald guy and send it anonymously to the police and say that he was the murderer. Would it be asking for too much hope that they could pin everything on Baldy before Drake got picked up or killed?

In the last five minutes of the drive, Drake contemplated how his father was involved. There's no way Drake would accept that his dad had been a part of the carnage of the last ten hours.

There had to be an explanation.

Drake pulled onto Jones Avenue. He edged along until the sign for Hunter Street came into view. He took the left and cruised up Hunter, carefully watching for movement of any kind. All the cars were parked on the right with little parking pass stickers purchased at Toronto City Hall on their windshields. As he passed each one, Drake checked for the parking passes. Any car without one didn't belong, but all twelve vehicles he passed had one. He also didn't see anyone sitting in any of the cars staking out his dad's place.

He made it to the end of Hunter Street, where he did a three-point turn and drove back down to park in front of his parents' home. After turning off his old Pontiac, Drake sat and studied the area. If anyone lie in wait, this would be the best time for him to bolt. He was still behind the wheel of his car. He could race out of there with a quick turn of the key. The last thing he wanted to do was get out and expose himself to a crazy gunman if one lingered in a bush somewhere.

A soft breeze wafted in through the open back window. He heard nothing from outside but the din of traffic from Jones Street. Hunter Street remained quiet, as it always did at twelve-thirty in the morning.

Satisfied that no one followed him and that no one knew where he was, Drake unlocked his door and stepped from the vehicle. He turned, locked the door, and shut it softly.

He made his way around the car, up the walkway, and to the front door without anything happening. He knocked on the front door of his parents' home. They would definitely be asleep at this hour, but before using the back door, as he did for years in high school, he had to try a few more times to make sure. He knocked louder and longer and then waited. Another glance around the front yard, the street, and his car told him he was alone. If he was being watched, they were hidden too well.

Drake walked down the steps and took the concrete path around the side of the house to the back. He flipped the latch on the gate and quietly opened it. If someone lie in wait, this would be a good spot. Undetected by the houses in the front and unseen by the houses in the back across the alley, an intruder could remain hidden there, waiting to pounce.

No intruder jumped him. No gunman fired at him, and no one tried to stop him as he moved a patio chair away from the sliding door that led into the kitchen.

The door was locked. If anyone attempted to open it, the door would remain steadfast. When he lifted the door an inch using the handle, it also lifted the catch, slipping it out of place when lowering the door back down. Unlocking it this way was something he'd been doing since high school.

He lifted the door with quiet precision and deft hands and eased it along its track.

Something about what he was doing felt too easy. An idea formed in his head. The bald guy had more purpose than framing a random person for murder. Drake's dad set up the meeting. Once the police had captured Drake, as the bald guy had wanted because he would've had limited foresight into Drake escaping, he had to know that Drake would explain everything. He'd start with his father, and they'd come and pick up his dad to sweat him, too. An investigation would ensue, and Drake would get a lawyer. In the eyes of a jury, doubt that Drake murdered the girl in apartment 1408 would've been established. A proper rape kit at the hospital would reveal no Drake Bellamy DNA anywhere.

That led Drake to believe the bald guy was up to something else—something deeper. But why had he been at Drake's apartment? He had to have been there when Drake was asleep on the couch. If the guy wanted him dead, he could've killed him right then.

That would explain why he missed when firing his weapon. He wasn't aiming to kill. His goal was to have the police called. Once they showed, all the pieces of the puzzle would fall together, and the authorities would know the name of the man in the dead girl's apartment in Scarborough.

But that took him back to square one. What would be the bald guy's end purpose if it was just to have Drake picked up by the cops? Nothing made sense. The only thing he figured from all of it was that the bald guy aimed to make Drake's life miserable. Or worse, he was trying to ruin his life completely.

Drake stepped into the dark kitchen and stopped. He listened for any kind of movement or other noises, but there was nothing. He couldn't even hear his mother's rhythmic breathing from upstairs, which was a common sound throughout the house unless her bedroom door was shut.

His parents bought the house when his mother was three months pregnant with Drake. He lived with his parents until he was twenty-one. For nine years, he'd been on his own. He knew every square inch and hiding spot in his twenty-one years of living in this home.

His parents' kitchen furniture hadn't changed in over seven years, so it was easy to navigate the table and chairs as he entered the center of the building, where he would find the stairwell.

He stopped to listen. Nothing.

He touched the banister and began taking each stair one at a time.

It wasn't a hot night, but sweat threatened to fall into his eyes. He wiped it away with his free hand. When he did, he smelled the orange Dead Head shirt he wore. It reeked of sweat and fear.

He reached the top of the stairs and saw his parents' bedroom door shut. That was unusual. When they were alone, they always left it open.

Now, he had two things to consider. If the bald guy's purpose was for Drake to be picked up by the cops, they were on their way here within the next half hour. They wouldn't drive from Mississauga. They would radio ahead, and other police officers would race to Hunter Street and surround his parents' house with him in it.

The other thing to consider was the closed door. There was a very high chance that someone was already here. Or had been here. It was odd for their bedroom door to be shut.

Did that mean something had happened to his parents? Was he about to enter another bedroom, discover more bodies, and have the police pull up out front?

Couldn't be. If that were the case, then who were these people? How could they know so much about him? Thinking back to an earlier evening, he could come up with no names or reasons for this assault on his person. He had no enemies to speak of, and as far as he remembered, he'd wronged no one.

Contemplation and deduction weren't getting him through the bedroom door to his father's bedside and the answers he desperately needed. It was also a form of procrastination.

The truth was, though, if he did walk into their bedroom and find anything other than his parents having a fitful sleep, he would go crazy. That would be the last straw. Bald Guy hadn't seen that side of Drake yet. He would stop at nothing to make sure the fucking asshole paid a steep price for his actions.

No one fucked with his parents.

With nothing left to lose, he strode briskly across the hardwood floor, grabbed the doorknob, and swung his parents' bedroom door wide open.

He shuffled in the room too fast and collided with something on the floor. His balance gone, Drake stumbled forward, waiting for the bed's footboard to crack open his skull. He hit the floor and stopped before stumbling as far as the bed. A sharp pain shot through his arm. He groaned as he rolled onto his back and reached for the wounded shoulder.

A soft light flickered on, illuminating the room into an amber existence.

"Dad?"

Drake rolled onto his side and made to stand but stopped when he saw what had tripped him. Someone had deliberately laid a suitcase on the floor two feet from the bedroom door.

Who would do such a stupid thing?

"Get up."

Drake turned his head so fast at the sound of the voice that his neck snapped.

"I said, get up. We haven't got much time."

A man sat in the corner of his parents' bedroom on his mother's reading chair. Years ago, she had put a recliner in the corner under a lamp so she could read into the evening on those nights when she suffered from insomnia. It also kept her close to Dad as she always professed that every hour she had left on this green earth had to be spent with her man, her rock.

The loss of Drake's normal life within the last twelve hours, coupled with almost being shot before coming here, fueled his anger. Seeing a stranger in his parents' bedroom was enough to drive him to violence. But seeing that stranger sitting in his mother's chair, the chair she may very well die in within the next few months, drove Drake over the cliff of absolute rage.

He got to his feet and started across the floor.

"Hold up," the man said. "Sit down on the bed ..."

His steps held purpose, his gait determined. Drake recognized the moment the man in the chair understood Drake's intentions.

Not three feet from him, Drake saw the man's arm snake down to his waistband and come back up with a gun held firm in his grip.

At the second the gun was leveled at Drake's face, he was on the last step that brought him an arm's length away.

With speed he wasn't aware he possessed, Drake swung with his right hand, smacking the weapon so hard that the gun was knocked from the man's grasp before he got his finger inside the trigger guard.

Drake allowed his right hand to continue on its path to the left after hitting the gun so he could wind up on the way back.

It all happened so fast that the guy in the chair had almost no time to respond. Drake's right hand came back across the man's face with a loud, resounding smack. The man's face shot sideways. Drake grabbed his shirt about the collar with both hands, half lifted him, and yelled an inch from his nose, "What have you done with my parents?" Spittle flew from his clenched teeth.

"Let me go, or your parents die. Worse than the cancer eating away at your mother, I assure you."

Drake mentally stumbled. A myriad of questions screamed through his consciousness. Who were these people, and how did they know so much about his family?

His breathing had taken on a raspy, guttural sound. Small strings of spit fought through his clenched teeth. He had never felt so much power and weakness at the same time. At that moment, he knew he could tear this man apart, but at the same time, he would be guilty of what the cops were hunting him for, and he would put his parents' lives in danger if what this guy said was true.

These people had a plan. If he continued this cat-and-mouse game fueled by rage, he would lose. He needed to regroup, think everything through, find their weaknesses, and get an ally in the police department. Find a lawyer. Buy a gun. Carry a knife. Buy pepper spray. He needed to do something to avoid these people always surprising him.

He released his grip and let the guy's shirt go.

"Where are my parents?"

The man got to his feet, walked over to the fallen gun, and retrieved it. To Drake's surprise, the guy put it back inside his waistband.

He turned to address Drake and smiled as he rubbed the side of his face.

"Allow me to introduce myself. My name is Attila, and I can see you haven't figured anything out yet, have you?"

"Is this where you tell me what's going on?"

The man raised his right index finger and waved it back and forth like he was telling a little boy that he had done wrong.

"No, no, no. You have to figure it out on your own. This goes deep. Very deep. It has been in the works for over a decade."

The man spoke with a slight accent. It wasn't one Drake could place readily, but it was one he recognized. The guy also resembled the other asshole with the snake tattoo.

He made a couple of guesses and assumptions in that instant.

"What did I do to your family that was so wrong? Why are you and your brother doing this?"

The man standing before him cocked his head to the side. His eyes narrowed as he stared back at Drake.

"I've never been to Europe," Drake continued. "As your name suggests, you're from Hungary. You and your brother and his fucking snake tattoo must have the wrong guy. You've made a big mistake."

Drake could tell by the stare that he was hitting every

note perfectly. Without protesting, the man confirmed everything Drake said. But what did that mean? It was true. He'd never been to Europe. So, how could he have wronged their family? Why him? What was he missing?

"You've been thinking about your situation. You have come up with a few theories." He stepped back in front of the chair. "I will tell you that you will pay dearly for what you did. No one can be allowed a free pass. Not for the crimes you committed. My brother Laszlo and I will see to it."

They really did have the wrong guy. There was no way he did anything severe enough to anyone to deserve this.

"Where are my parents? What have you done with them?"

"They're safe. We have no beef with them. In days when this is all over, they will be returned to their lives completely unharmed. I knew you would come here to ask questions of your father. I thought it would give us a chance to talk."

"There's nothing to talk about. You and your brother are murderers."

The guy raised his finger and waved it back and forth.

"It is not I who is the murderer. It is you."

What was he saying? Drake hadn't killed anyone. "Now I'm *convinced* you have the wrong guy. Turn yourselves in, and we'll consider this a little case of mistaken identity."

The man cleared his throat and spat a disgusting glob of phlegm on the floor in front of Drake's shoes.

"You stand before me only because I want you to suffer. Otherwise, you would already be dead. Don't push me. I'm the wrong guy to push."

Drake stepped back. He was out of his element, and he knew it. His anger was wearing off.

The man stared with such malevolence that Drake almost looked away.

"This will all be over soon. Your parents will survive, but what happens to you may kill them. My brother and I have a few more surprises in store."

Drake took another step backward. "Why me? You haven't explained what I did to you. Tell me what it is, and maybe I can fix it."

"There is no fixing what you did. There is only fixing you because of it."

The man stepped closer, causing Drake to move away again. He had cleared the end of the bed and was walking backward, the bedroom door close.

A distant police siren wailed in the night.

"The police will be here shortly. Go with them. Tell them anything you want about my brother and me. It won't matter. You will spend the rest of your life in prison being somebody's bitch. Your life is over, Drake Bellamy. Without murdering you, I have killed you."

On his last word, the man lunged forward. Out of reflex, Drake jumped back and lost his balance as he hit the luggage piece on the floor with his heel.

This time, the floor collided with his tailbone hard, making him gasp at the sudden pain.

The man was on him in seconds. Three punches landed on either side of his face. With each blow, Drake heard the man grunt a few words in another language—Hungarian.

It was over as fast as it started. He rolled into a ball and breathed through his mouth, willing the pain to subside. Both cheeks were inflamed and felt larger than they were.

His mind reeled. He wondered where the man was.

Footsteps down the hallway confirmed that he had left the bedroom. Drake heard the man clomping down the stairs. The police sirens were very close.

Even though he wanted to curl into a ball until it all went away, Drake angled himself to a sitting position. He got to his feet and listened. The sirens sounded like they were right outside.

He had a moment to decide. Stop running, give himself up, or try to leave undetected and attempt to figure everything out on his own.

In that moment of indecision, he ran. To not run would be to give in not just to the police but also to the two brothers terrorizing him. That's what they wanted. Whatever they had against him, both men were determined to see him incarcerated. There was a reason for that. Drake still didn't know why, but he needed to figure it out before he went down.

The police could wait. Jail could wait. It would always be there when this was over. Hopefully, he could flip this on their heads, and the asshole brothers would be the ones spending time in jail.

He hit the stairs running, taking them two at a time. Red lights flashed through the front windows. The police were already there.

He ran to the back, through the kitchen, and to the sliding door. A quick scan revealed no one in the rear of the house yet. He slid the door open and eased out onto the patio where he had spent many years having summer barbecues and parties. The memories flooded back, and he was thinking about his parents again and what might be happening to them. Water covered his vision as his eyes teared up at the thought of losing all he held close because two assholes got the wrong guy.

He couldn't get to his car out front. All he had was his wallet, cell phone, and knowledge of the area. He ran through the yard and hit the back fence in seconds. The gate opened from the inside. He flicked the latch and barreled through it, but not before noticing someone watching him.

Drake slowed to see if it was the man from his parents' bedroom. It wasn't. It was a woman. She stood in the shadows of a neighbor's shed. He could only discern her figure and the long flowing hair.

With each step, he moved away from her as more noises came from the front of his parents' house.

Finally, he turned and ran to the end of the alley. With a quick left and up a small side street, Drake made it to the park that would lead him out to the Danforth by a 7-Eleven convenience store.

The woman disturbed him the most after all that he'd gone through.

Something about her was familiar. It felt like a buried memory. One that called out to him and continued to try to get noticed.

Whatever it was, it didn't involve murder. He'd remember a detail like that. There was no way he had ever done any real harm to anyone. If he had, why wasn't the law after him? Because he hadn't done anything to anyone.

But that was going to change.

The brothers needed to be taught a lesson.

What did it matter now? Drake had lost everything the way things were. It was only a matter of time before the police picked him up. The potential for him to spend the rest of his life in jail for a murder he didn't commit was quite high.

He refused to spend time locked up for something he didn't do.

At least killing those two fucking brothers would make things more realistic.

Any jury would agree, he thought and laughed at his rationale as he ran past an all-night convenience store.

Chapter 4

DRAKE WAS FINISHED WITH being predictable. The European brothers wouldn't figure out what he was up to next. From then on, he was going to surprise them.

He had to keep moving and keep thinking. Soon, a piece of the puzzle would fall into place, and he'd be one step closer to figuring everything out.

Drake entered the 7-Eleven and headed for the side rack. It was quiet at this late hour. Only one man stood off to the side, flipping through a magazine. He hadn't looked up when Drake walked in.

In a corner beside the Big Gulp machine sat a hat rack featuring caps with slogans about drinking, smoking, and sex acts. Drake grabbed a Toronto Maple Leafs hat and walked to the counter. He quickly glanced at the newspapers and saw that one had the police artist's sketch of his face on the front cover.

That was fast.

The chance the pierced, tattooed, and purple-haired clerk would put it all together was slim. The clerk probably didn't read newspapers.

Drake set the cap on the counter and reached for his money.

"Do you ever read The Toronto Star newspaper?" Drake asked.

The clerk looked at him sideways and then flipped his hair back out of his face in an exaggerated head toss.

"No, dude. You serious?"

"Not really. How much for the hat?"

"Eleven and a half."

Drake paid him with a twenty, got the change, and headed for the door. He ripped off the price tag and placed the hat on his head.

At the door, he turned back to the clerk who was watching him. No doubt, thinking *he* was the weirdo.

"You know, working the night shift, you really should read the newspapers or at least watch the news. You never know who might walk in on your shift."

Drake turned and left, leaving the kid with a look of bewilderment on his face. He crossed the street and started up the Danforth, heading for the Coffee Time Donut Shop one city block away.

He looked back before he lost sight of the interior of the 7-Eleven. The clerk was on the customer side of the counter, a newspaper in his hand, mouth wide open.

Good, Drake thought. *Just what I wanted.*

He hustled up the street with the baseball cap lowered to just over his eyes. He felt fully alive for the first time in a long time. The five-hour nap earlier in his apartment had rejuvenated him. It felt like one in the afternoon and not one in the morning.

Just as he suspected, a yellow cab sat in front of Coffee Time. He slowed at the corner of Jones Avenue to ensure no cops were in sight. A cruiser sat parked about five hundred meters down on Jones. But that was it. There were no cops in the donut shop.

Drake crossed Jones and entered the coffee shop. He approached the taxi driver at his booth, nursing a large black coffee.

"That your cab?" he asked.

"Yeah," the cabbie said without looking up.

"Can you take me to the Valhalla Inn off the East Mall?"

"I'm off duty. Get the clerk to call you another one."

Drake shook his head. "I need you. How much?"

The cabbie looked up. "I said I'm off duty. Buzz off."

Drake sat at the man's table opposite him. The cabbie leaned back, unsure of what to expect.

"Look, this is serious," Drake said. "I just received a call from my girl. She's really fucking hot." Drake used his hands to demonstrate her figure. "She called me saying she was lonely and shit. She already paid for a hotel room. I'm wasting time here. I need to be there as fast as I can, and at this time of night, I could lose a half hour or more waiting for another cab." He pulled out his wallet. "Look, the ride would be ten to fifteen minutes, tops. It would be thirty bucks, at least. Drive me there, and I will give you one hundred dollars. Meter or no meter. Deal?"

The cabbie looked at the hundred being offered and took another sip of his coffee.

He didn't protest right away, which meant he had him.

"You'd do the same for a twenty-two-year-old college girl with a perfect body. I need to get to the Valhalla Inn. Do a brother a favor."

The cabbie nodded. "Okay, one hundred bucks. No meter."

"Deal." Drake shot his hand out to shake the cabbie's. He pulled it back as the cab driver stood and headed for the door, his hand untouched.

Drake followed.

They got in the taxi, and the cabbie asked for the money upfront. Drake passed it forward to the front seat.

Seconds later, they were racing toward the Don Valley Parkway along the Danforth. At this late hour, the highway was mostly empty. They made good time along the Gardiner and up the 427. The cabbie exited onto the East Mall without a word.

The Valhalla Inn came into view. Drake leaned forward and asked, "Do you read the newspapers?"

"Yeah, all the time. Sitting in a cab all day, you gotta read somethin'."

"How about the news on TV?"

"When I get the chance. Why?"

They pulled into the main hotel entrance. "Just wondering if you recognized me."

The cabbie looked at him in the rearview mirror. "Should I?"

"No reason." Jake shrugged. "You will be asked about this trip by the cops. I would advise you to tell the truth. Tell them I talked you into taking this ride after your shift with the meter off. It'll look better that way."

The cab slowed and then stopped ten meters from the entrance to the hotel.

"Why? Who are you?" The cab driver's voice sounded hesitant and cautious.

"You'll know when you read the morning papers."

Drake opened the door and jumped from the cab. The taxi sped away, the door slamming shut.

Perfect, Drake thought.

He hustled away from the Valhalla Inn and into the darkness of the shrubbery beyond the parking area. He kept his movements confined to when vehicular traffic in the area was absent. He was exposed only when walking across the Bloor Street bridge.

He needed a hotel. Somewhere that took cash and didn't need ID. He knew where they were since he had lived in Toronto his entire life.

After he crossed the Bloor Street bridge, he kept to the shadows again as he ran down The West Mall. He dropped down Westmall Crescent and onto Dundas, where he immediately saw the little fires from the lamp posts at La Castile Restaurant. Behind the restaurant was the Super 5 Inn.

As he passed La Castile, he took off the baseball cap and folded the bill in half until it squeezed into the back pocket of his jeans. Then he removed the Dead Head T-shirt, folded it inside out, and put it back on. When the police sent out a description on the news in the morning based on the eyewitness statements of the 7-Eleven clerk and the cabbie, he didn't want the hotel clerk readily recognizing him.

He entered the front and handed the clerk, who wore a turban and a very thick black beard, two twenties. He received a room key and headed upstairs.

The room was standard and exactly what Drake needed for the night. He hit the bed hard, the exhaustion settling in.

His plan worked perfectly. No one knew where he was. He had a bed and a shower for the morning. All he needed next was a shave and a change of clothes. That could be accomplished in the morning, too.

The police would scour the area near his parents' home and come up empty-handed until they reached the 7-Eleven. Unless the clerk called them first, which Drake doubted as he probably had a few priors himself.

The police would question the clerk, and security cameras would show that Drake was wearing the orange Dead Head T-shirt, but now he had added a Toronto Maple Leaf baseball cap to his disguise.

They would be looking for someone Drake wouldn't resemble in the morning.

The cabbie might call it in. But even if he did, the same description would corroborate the store clerk's story. Also, they would search every room of the Valhalla Inn. There were a considerable number of hotels in the area. They couldn't possibly search each one in time, and he was over ten blocks away in a room without a name on any computer. In six hours, he would be gone and looking completely different.

Then, he could figure out his next step. He had an idea of what he wanted to do, but it would take some luck and planning on his part. He would also need patience.

Drake rolled to the side and wondered why he didn't look in the mirror when he got to the room. It would have been his best chance to see what that asshole had done to his face.

Probably nothing but red marks and bruising, but he still needed to check. Getting a black eye right now could hurt his chances of staying disguised.

As he drifted off to sleep, he heard the guy at his parents' house talking in his head—that Hungarian accent again.

Then the answer came to him. He shot up in bed.

"No way," he whispered to the empty room. "I can't believe it. I *won't* believe it."

Hungarian.

Monika was Hungarian.

Did he know any other Hungarians?

Only Monika from high school. His old girlfriend. The one who disappeared. She had been found in Budapest. She had broken his heart. When she ran, four months before they were to elope, she had taken his heart with her. It had been twelve years since she'd left. That was one of the last times he had heard the harsh sound of a Hungarian accent.

And now he'd heard it again. In his parents' house. By the very people who were terrorizing him.

Could the last twenty-four hours have anything to do with Monika? Attila said something about the plan being ten years in the making.

Nothing connected or seemed plausible at all, and it was the thinnest idea he had. But it was all he had. Two men show up with Hungarian accents. They talk about how this was in the works for over ten years. They know everything about him. Where he lives, where his parents live, and that his mother needs medical weed. They probably got his dad to call him with the address that set him up in the first place.

Everything seemed much clearer and much easier to swallow based on that thought pattern. It had to have something to do with Monika.

And who was the strange woman watching him run in the alley behind his parents' house? Could that have been Monika? Was he stretching events to make them work into a plausible scenario?

He had to meet up with Avery Hammond.

In the morning, he would visit Avery to see what he remembered about that fateful night when Monika left his life forever.

Chapter 5

DRAKE WOKE WITH A start. After a quick breath, he sat up fast and checked the time: 9:14 a.m. Checkout was at eleven.

He used the bathroom and dressed in yesterday's clothes. The television was quite old, but it worked. On *City Pulse 24*, he only had to wait five minutes before he got an update on his situation.

The update proved his suspicion was correct. He was being set up.

Drake fell back on the bed, completely spent.

Another body had been discovered. A female, aged twenty-nine. The body was discovered in the bedroom of the home of one Drake Bellamy. The same man police were looking for to question about the brutal murder of Anne Keeley in an apartment building on Victoria Park Avenue in Scarborough. Police have issued another urgent alert that they need to apprehend Mr. Bellamy and that he is considered armed and dangerous. Do not approach.

The news channel described an orange T-shirt and a baseball cap with the Toronto Maple Leaf's logo on it. He had been attempting to disguise his appearance, but some tips came in throughout the evening that Drake Bellamy was in the Etobicoke area.

More on the report would be coming at noon as Toronto Police would hold a press conference with the officer in charge of the case, Spencer Milton.

Drake had heard enough. He left the hotel room key on the bureau, entered the corridor, and walked to the back end of the motel to avoid the front. By way of the back stairwell, Drake exited the Super 5 Inn and walked around the back and behind the restaurant next door.

In minutes, he was walking down The West Mall toward Sherway Gardens. He had a plan and knew how to execute it. No cops were in sight, and he'd seen no police cars out front of the Super 5 Inn. They had no idea where he was, and he intended to keep it that way.

Unless he figured out what was going on, his life was forfeit. Two days ago, he was deciding what movie to see at the theater and what to eat for dinner. Such mundane tasks compared to the choices he had to make now.

Once in the Sherway Gardens Shopping Mall, he would have what he needed. Then, he would call Spencer Milton, the officer in charge. He would offer him a deal, and once Spencer promised fair treatment, Drake would turn himself in.

Sherway Gardens came into view. The sun glinted off the cars racing along The Queensway. He glanced upward and couldn't detect a single cloud in the sky. Normally, it was a perfect day for a round of golf at his favorite Yonge Street course or Kleinburg, but that felt like a lifetime away. Would he ever be able to golf again, or would he rot in jail? Would this bullshit remove his freedoms permanently?

That's what he had to avoid. Whoever these people were, Drake felt a sense of power around dealing with what had happened. He needed to find his parents, too. So far, the Hungarian men had proven that they either kill or terrorize the people they get close to. When this was over, Drake wouldn't be rotting in a prison cell as they wanted. It would be the two of them rotting in the dirt.

He crossed The Queensway and entered Sherway Gardens at the doors that lead into The Bay, where he found a ten-dollar shirt that fit perfectly. The changing rooms weren't in use this early. He entered one, changed, and balled up the orange Dead Head shirt to toss into the garbage. At the till, he paid and headed to the beard trimmers and shavers section sporting his new collared shirt. On the way over, he slowed near a garbage receptacle and dropped the Dead Head shirt inside. He felt properly disguised now that the orange shirt was gone.

Next, he found a shaver that would do what he needed. At the closest counter, he paid cash and headed for The Bay's washroom.

Beside the men's and women's bathroom doors sat a separate entrance for the handicapped washroom. He entered it and locked the door behind him. In the single bathroom, he could do what he needed without interruption.

After unwrapping the new shaver, he plugged it in and shaved his head by running a stripe down the middle. Moments later, he admired the bald pate and smiled at what

Snake Head would think when he saw him again.

Next, he applied the beard trimmer to the shaver and shaved his face, leaving a thin goatee behind. With the bald head, goatee, and new collared shirt, Drake looked completely different from the guy sporting a baseball cap and an orange Dead Head T-shirt. He was unrecognizable.

He threw everything he'd used in the bathroom garbage and opened the door slowly. After leaving the washroom, he walked through the store feeling invisible.

Soon after, he was in the food court, smelling the aromas. He ordered a five-taco deal at Taco Bell and then devoured them. On the last one, a man came up the stairs thirty meters from him and headed his way. He didn't pay special attention to Drake as he scanned everyone's face, looking for someone.

Five meters from Drake, the man looked directly at him, slowed his pace, and stopped by Drake's table.

Drake stopped chewing and lowered the taco. He gripped the table's edge and prepared to launch from his seat.

The stranger pointed at Drake's head.

"You're bleeding," he said.

Drake lifted a hand and touched the skin in the area the guy gestured at. His hand came away with blood on it.

"Thanks," he said, his voice deeper than he intended. "Must've cut it this morning while shaving."

"No problem," the guy said and walked away.

Drake watched him go as he let his heart return to a normal rhythm.

He had to leave. The mall was too populated. Testing his disguise held no benefits. He dropped the used wrappings into the garbage and returned to the main mall area.

In ten minutes, he had bought a small digital camera and was on his way to the Apple Store, where he got a clerk to log him onto the internet. Once online, he had located two A. Hammonds that were a plausible fit for his old high school friend. One lived in North York, the other on High Street in south Mississauga, off Hurontario Street. That A. Hammond was closer and sounded more like the Avery he remembered, as The Port Credit area was more expensive and Avery had money.

Drake left the mall by a side door, where he found a bank of pay phones. He called a cab and waited in the shelter of the double doors.

The taxi arrived and took him to the bottom of Hurontario, where he got out and walked away from High Street until the cab was out of sight.

Then he returned and went to the small apartment building where he hoped to find Hammond.

When Monika left for Budapest all those years ago, Avery was there, and the police were questioning Drake like he'd done something to her. Avery had been there when Drake woke up in the hospital, and no one knew what had happened, how he received his injuries, or even how he got to the hospital.

It had been a dark time in his life. There were too many unknowns, and the police didn't buy it. By the time Monika had been found alive and well in Budapest, and the questioning of Drake had ceased, he had just wanted to forget. To let everything go and start anew.

They had planned to elope. Then, he was in the hospital with injuries and a mild concussion, and she was in Europe.

Now, twelve years later, two Hungarian men had raped

and killed two women and framed Drake for the murders with the precision of a brain surgeon.

It had to be connected somehow because it was all he had to go on.

The back of the building offered no access without a key. He walked around to the front and scanned the names on the buzzer board. Avery Hammond, apartment 404.

Drake stepped out of the front door and headed to the back again. He would wait it out. As soon as someone left from inside the building, heading to their car, he would grab the door before it closed.

He didn't have to wait long.

The door opened, and a woman stepped out. He rushed into action, fumbling with his keys and grabbing the door simultaneously.

"Thanks," he said and ran in. The woman didn't look back.

He took the stairs to the fourth floor and entered the hallway. At least this hall didn't smell as bad as the building in Victoria Park. It was cool as the air conditioners pumped cold air through vents above his head.

He strolled along until he stood in front of Avery's apartment door. Still unsure if this was the apartment of the Avery he knew and not sure how a reunion after twelve years would go, Drake tentatively knocked on the door.

Footsteps approached from the inside.

A lock snapped, and he could hear a chain unraveling.

The door opened, and he instantly recognized his old high school buddy.

What he didn't recognize was the gun in Avery's hand.

Avery lifted the weapon and placed the barrel against

Drake's forehead. Drake felt Avery's nervousness through the barrel's shaking against his skin. Drake had to tighten several muscles to keep his bladder together.

"I should kill you right now, right here," Avery said, "for what you did. Give me one good reason not to kill you. Give me something, or I swear you are on your last breath."

The gun clicked.

Chapter 6

Drake stepped back, stunned. The gun moved with him. If Avery had seen the news, why not tell him to leave? Or call the police? Why kill him?

"Whatever you think I've done, I assure you I didn't do it," Drake said.

He had slept well. Rejuvenated and with his appearance so drastically altered, he felt like he had the upper hand in his situation. He had no idea he'd be facing a gun.

"Not good enough," Avery said. "I should kill you before you kill me."

"What?" *What was he talking about?* "I'm not here to kill you."

"Tell me the truth." Avery stepped back into his apartment, the gun moving away from Drake's forehead. "Just tell me."

Drake raised his hands out to the side and, in an

exasperated voice, said, "Why would I want to kill *you*?" He blinked, swallowed involuntarily, then asked, "Look, can we continue talking inside? What if someone sees us like this?"

"They'd call the police, and you would be taken in. Your name is all over the news. You need to pay for what you did."

Drake saw his old friend go through a series of conflicting emotions all at the same time. Avery's eyes watered, and his gun hand shook. If Drake didn't get the gun pointed elsewhere fast, he was sure he'd be shot accidentally.

Avery used his free hand to wipe his wet eyes. Then he gestured with the gun for Drake to enter.

"One stupid move, and I will put a bullet in you."

Drake walked past him and stepped into Avery's living room.

From behind him, Avery asked, "Are you packing?"

"Packing? Like as in carrying a weapon?"

Avery held his gun at arm's length, pointed in Drake's direction, and quickly turned to look out his door in the outside hallway. Then he shut the door and locked it.

He turned back at Drake. "Yes. Are you carrying a gun?"

"No, I am not," Drake said, enunciating each word. He glared at him. "I came here to talk to you about what happened the night I was found and taken to the hospital. Back in high school—"

"I know what you're talking about." Avery walked by, giving Drake a wide berth as if he had a communicable disease. He moved to a recliner in the corner and sat hard. His gun hand dropped to the armrest as he wiped at his wet eyes again. "Is that what you said to them before you killed them? I want to talk about that night in high school?"

Drake's mind drew a blank. He had no idea what Avery

was talking about. It seemed like everything he knew about people kept changing. Yesterday, all he wanted was a little medical weed for his mother. And now his parents were missing, two people had been found dead, and the police were looking for him. To top it off, after a decade, his best friend from high school was having a nervous breakdown with a gun and talking about nothing that made sense.

"I need to be honest with you, Avery," Drake said. He kept his hands up and walked around the edge of the couch to take a seat. "I have zero idea what's happening here. We were best friends in high school. You were there for me that terrible night. I recently met two men who might be connected to that night, and I thought I could try to find you and ask what you might remember. I had no idea this was such a bad time."

Avery tilted his head sideways as he seemed to be working things out. "Are you for real?"

"Yes, I'm for real. Actually, I think I'm the only one who is acting normal anymore."

"So you kill two people, disguise yourself by shaving your head, and run from the cops after meeting a couple of people connected to your past. Then you come over here to catch up on old times? There's got to be something else. It's not an accident you're here, and I think I know why you came."

Drake leaned into the couch and steepled his hands to keep them visible to Avery.

"Why am I here then, Avery? You tell me."

"To kill me, too."

"Okay. Why would I do that?"

"Revenge."

"Revenge? I'm not following. You were my best friend. What possible motivation would I have to conjure up revenge?"

"Maybe your memory returned? Maybe you figured out what happened? Someone could've told you. Perhaps you just decided to fix things? I have no fucking idea, but I can tell you that it is the worst way to go about it."

"You know, Avery, I don't remember you this way."

"What way?"

"Fucked in the head. You keep talking in circles. I have no idea what you're talking about. What could someone have told me?"

Avery narrowed his eyes. He wore a white wife-beater shirt that revealed long drooping sweat stains under the arms. His green shorts were also stained like he'd spilled beer on them. Either that, or he pissed himself from here to Sunday.

It was a lot to take in, but Drake was getting that Avery had been messed up for some time. He acted like he had a shot of rabies, all wild-eyed and crazy.

"So, the invincible Drake Bellamy has no idea what I'm talking about, eh? No idea that the only reason you were in the hospital back then was me? I'm the one who kicked you in the head hard enough to knock the memories out."

Drake dropped his hands. His leg tapped up and down. "How is that possible?" He blinked, then frowned. "I don't understand."

"Either you're a good actor, or you really don't know."

"Avery, just tell me what I'm missing. You're the one with the fucking gun. Tell me."

Drake recognized his swear trigger. The angrier he got, the more of a gutter mouth he had.

"I'm the one who hit you in the head that night." Avery wiped his forehead. "You wouldn't stay down."

"How come this is the first I'm hearing about it? Have you told the police?"

"Do you think I'm stupid? You're the only one I've told. Two other people know because they were there, but you're the only one I've told."

Completely unsure why his best friend would've hurt him the way he did, Drake asked, "What two people?"

"Kory and, of course, Monika."

That hit him hard. He was surprised again.

"Monika? She went missing. How could she know anything?"

"She was why we were there, to begin with."

"I'm not following. Where were we, and why were all four of us there?"

Avery lifted his gun and checked something on it. Then he rested it back down, aimed at Drake.

"You know," Drake said. "I'm not real comfortable with that thing pointed at me. I'm not armed, and I didn't come here to do anything other than talk, so you can put it away or aim it someplace else."

"Who are you trying to kid? Drake, my old friend, you are not leaving this apartment alive. There's no way. Not after what you did to those innocent girls."

Drake's stomach dropped a foot. Fear gripped his internal organs.

"I didn't do anything to those girls."

"Tell that to a jury. Oh, wait, there won't be one. You're only getting a judge: me."

"Then tell me why. At least give me that. Explain it all

while I sit here being all harmless and shit. Make it a last request. Tell me everything you know."

"You really are a stupid shit, aren't you? The cards you sent in the mail. The ones with the subtle hints and the dates that were dead on. If that wasn't you, then I don't know who it was because only you could know that shit. I checked with Kory. He got the cards, too. Today's date was on my card."

Drake looked around the room. Avery's apartment seemed normal in every way. A large flat-screen TV. A matching loveseat, couch, and chair with an extra recliner in the corner, the one Avery currently occupied. Pictures on the wall. A fern in another corner by the balcony door. Yet it all seemed surreal as Avery talked in doublespeak.

Drake looked back at Avery. "Are you high?"

"No, I've had a few drinks, but no drugs. I never did drugs."

"You sound high to me."

"I'm not. I need to kill you to stay alive so that I won't get high on such a momentous day."

"Tell me, Avery, why do you have to kill me?"

"Because everything you said in the cards you mailed Kory and me has come true."

Drake's anger rose again. "I haven't sent you any fucking cards! What the shit are you talking about?" He half lifted off the couch.

"Sit the fuck back down, or I will shoot you now, and you won't get that last request you asked for."

Drake eased back onto the couch but remained on the edge of the cushion.

"I received a birthday card two months ago, even though it wasn't my birthday." Avery wiped his forehead. "The first card was tame. All it said was someone close to me would suffer for what I did. I had no idea what that meant. I thought back to who I might have wronged. I called a few people. I talked to my parents in Alberta. After two weeks, I let it go, thinking it was a prank. Then you sent another card."

"I didn't send any fucking cards to anyone."

"Whatever. I received another one saying that the date had been picked and that a person close to me would be raped, beaten, and then killed. The day after, it would be my turn."

Something is very wrong here.

Drake tried to place events in the right order. This was all about something Avery had done, and whoever was orchestrating it was going after people Avery knew, like Kory and Drake.

"So naturally, when you heard about Anne Keeley, you thought today would be your turn? Did you even know Anne?"

"We were engaged," Avery said. He choked up, then added, "Anne and I were planning a September wedding. And now she's dead because of you."

Drake sat back, shocked at the news. After a moment, he found his voice.

"Avery, I didn't do what you think I did. I'm being set up. The same people doing this to you and Anne are doing it to me. They kidnapped my parents and had my dad call me with an address. My mother has cancer, and I was told to go to an apartment building on Victoria Park. I was supposed to buy medical weed for my mother. Instead, I found a dead woman in the bedroom. I barely escaped. When I got home, they were in my apartment. I just found out this morning that the police found another dead body in my bedroom. You gotta believe me. I have nothing to do with this."

"Then why run?" Avery asked. "Why not tell the police everything?"

"Because I didn't want to go through … the truth is, I'm scared. I've never been busted before, and I didn't want to go down for trying to buy weed for my sick mother. Then, when I saw the dead body, I panicked. I wasn't going to get a murder charge against me for what the bald guy did. No way."

"Bald guy? What bald guy?"

"His name is Laszlo, and his brother's name is Attila. I don't know much other than the bald guy has a snake—"

"Tattoo," Avery finished for him.

"Yes. Have you met him?"

"I noticed him hanging around the building in the last few weeks near the little Korean convenience store across the street. I'd never seen him before. I became more paranoid once I started receiving the cards, watching my back."

So it was true. The Hungarians, most likely connected to Monika, were framing Drake and going after Kory and Avery. But why? What would motivate Monika to do such horrible things if Monika was involved?

Avery started talking again. "Let's suppose for a minute that what you're saying is true, and you didn't send the cards, and you didn't kill anyone. If not you, then who? Last I heard, over ten years ago, Monika was safe in Budapest. I connected it to the night of the struggle because of all the bad things I'd done that night. Seeing your name in the news and hearing that Anne was dead …"

Avery stopped as a flood of tears wracked his body. He

leaned forward and gripped his gut. Drake thought about disarming Avery. He would need to if he wanted to walk away from the apartment.

Avery glanced up quickly, his eyes a deep red and covered in tears.

"Don't even think. Just sit there and stay fucking still. For what you did to Anne, I will put a bullet up the tip of your cock and fire until your ass is the size of a watermelon. Do not fuck with me."

That convinced Drake. He sat back and waited. After a minute, Avery composed himself. He wiped more sweat off his brow and started talking again.

"I know Kory didn't send me the cards, and not because he was getting them, too. He could easily do that as a diversion. No, I know he wasn't involved for two reasons. One, that night was his idea. It was meant to scare you. Rough you up for fun. The other reason is he's dying in the hospital. What would he do, use his wheelchair to run me down?"

"Rough me up? Scare me? Why? What really happened that night? And what is Kory dying of? I haven't heard anything on Facebook. I still have a few friends from that era, and we stay connected."

"Kory is in the Princess Margaret Cancer Hospital downtown. He needs a liver transplant. He was admitted again four or five days ago for observation. But what does that matter? This has gone on way too long. You're stalling."

Drake raised his eyebrows and motioned with a finger to wait. Then, he slowly lowered his hand to the pocket that held the camera. With another look at Avery, he eased the camera out and set it on the couch beside him, where it moved a little, then rested between the cushions.

He used both hands to pat himself down.

"See, Avery. I pose no threat. I'm not wired, and I have no weapon. Only a camera and my wallet in this pocket." He pointed at his right front pocket. He didn't mention his cell phone in the back pocket.

"Why are you walking around with a camera?"

"The bald guy we spoke of earlier and his brother is why. I want to get a photo of them to send to the newspapers or the cops. I have no idea how to collect evidence, so I thought this might be a start. At least it would make them real. Maybe someone at the apartment in Scarborough or my place will recognize them. Now that you can see I'm not armed, and I'm telling you, as an old friend, that I'm not here to do you any harm, tell me more. I'm not stalling."

Avery appeared to mull it over. Drake waited, but he didn't have to wait long.

"Kory has a few health problems. He has a rare, advanced form of Hepatitis C. I've visited him several times and discovered that the virus persists in the liver in eighty-five percent of those infected. His was advanced. He developed problems with his liver and needs a transplant. They haven't found one yet. For the most part, he spends his time at home with a pager, but he recently went back to the hospital because he looked pretty jaundiced. Even then, I understand the virus recurs after transplant anyway."

Drake cut in, "So there's no hope for him?"

Avery shook his head and bit his lower lip. "We stayed close after high school. But now he's dying. He couldn't abstain from alcohol, which was recommended in his condition. The guy drinks hardcore."

"Go back a bit. What was that part about roughing me up? Why would you do that? You were my best friend. You stayed with me in the hospital, and now I'm finding out it was you who put me there."

Avery looked at the gun, then back to Drake. "You remember how hot Monika was. Kory and I both thought we'd get a chance with her. When you two started dating, we figured it wouldn't last. But then you told me you were going to take off and get married. I knew you were going to the lake that night to park, so Kory thought we should show up and scare you a little. We were pretty toasted, and really, it was meant to mess with Monika more than you. But you had to try and be a hero. And Monika was a tough bitch. I remember she took a swing at Kory and knocked him down. You dove for him, and I couldn't stop you, so I kicked you in the head. In my drunken state, I didn't know how hard I hit you. The rest is a blur. Monika was gone in the morning, and you were in the hospital. I stayed close to your bedside in case you started to remember anything. You never did. I felt like shit. The rest is history."

Avery lifted the gun.

"But now Kory's girlfriend and my girlfriend are dead, and we both have cards saying that I will die today. I don't know what Kory's card says about him. Haven't talked to him in about a week."

It all hit Drake in a rush. The bald guy had been watching Avery. Cards were mailed with dates. Their two girlfriends were killed because of whatever they did that night.

"What did you two do to Monika after I was knocked out?"

Avery looked away.

"What did you do?" Drake asked again.

Avery met his eyes. "I have lived with it and died inside a thousand times."

"What the fuck did you do?" Drake fought the urge to jump from the couch.

"It was mostly Kory. He held her down." Avery stopped and wiped his eyes. "She was wearing a dress. I looked at you and saw blood coming from the side of your head. You were out cold. I was scared. When I looked back at Monika, she was staring at me and crying, the fight gone out of her. Kory was pumping between her legs. I watched him in stunned silence. Then, all I remember was he told me we were in this together …"

"You didn't?" Drake said, his teeth clenched.

"See how angry you're getting? What would you have done?"

"Killed you."

"Exactly. Now you see how it adds up?" Avery instantly changed, his face narrowing. "You don't fucking know how it was. I wanted Monika. When she came to our school, I thought she'd be mine. Then you snatched her up, and you were going to *fucking* marry her. I wanted one hit off that before my best friend owned it. Of course, I raped her, you fucking idiot. I loved it and would've done it again and again, so fuck you. Don't judge me." He paused to breathe deeply, his chest expanding with the breath. "That's why Kory and I figured it was you after us with the cards. Then the police announced the two dead girls and that they were looking for you. They even came and talked to me about it. I'm not stupid. I know you're here to kill me."

"I didn't want to kill you when I knocked on your door,

but I'd like to now."

Avery stood and walked over to his apartment door. He looked through the peephole, tried the bolt, and then turned back to Drake.

"Get up," Avery ordered.

"No. Tell me what you did with Monika after that. Which one of you killed her? You would've had to. Otherwise, why didn't *she* say anything?"

"We didn't kill her. She went home to Hungary."

"Then why did she leave and remain silent? She wouldn't have done that. She was too tough. She would've gone to the police."

"We don't know."

"How did it end?" Drake asked. "At least tell me that."

"When we were finished, Kory rolled her over the cliff. You remember the hundred-foot drop in that area down to the rocky shore of Lake Ontario. It ended that night. We had no idea if she survived or not, but who could? We were sure she was dead. Then we heard she was in Hungary. Nothing happened again until I received the first card in the mail. Now, get up and walk to the bathroom. We're done here."

Drake stood and put both hands up, palms out in front of him. "Okay, right now, you have to listen to me. Those two men who have been terrorizing me have a strong Hungarian accent. Everything that has happened stems back to that night. I'm sure of it. Why they're framing me, I don't know because I didn't hurt her. I had nothing to do with this. One thing is for sure: I didn't come here to kill you. That means they are on their way here now. It wasn't me who sent you any cards."

"That's bullshit. For all I know, you hired the bald guy to

keep tabs on me in case I left town."

"Suppose I'm right." Drake lowered his hands. "Humor me for a sec. Snake Head shot at me. I met Attila at my parents' house. At either time, they could've killed me. But they kept me alive. Monika and I were in love, but she would blame me for not protecting her, so she wanted me to suffer as she did. This is something that won't go away. I will live with what has happened in the last twenty-four hours for the rest of my life. But with you and Kory, it's different. She took away your women as you took mine. Now, you two must pay the ultimate price. That sounds like a good reason for why the cards were sent." He paused and raised a finger. "But here's the catch. They need me alive. If they knew you would kill me, they would stop you. That means they are already here. Somewhere close and waiting to pounce. Avery, you need to leave with me. You need to run, or you will be killed."

Avery smiled. "I remember that about you. How you always fucked around with wild and stupid stories. Nice try, asshole. You die today, not me. Then it's all over. Monika has not traveled back to Canada to murder people from high school or their girlfriends. Good theory, but it doesn't work. Now, start walking."

Avery pointed toward the hall that led to the bathroom. Drake took a step forward, moving slowly down the hall. Avery motioned for him to enter the bedroom and then the attached bathroom.

When Drake entered the bathroom, he saw what Avery had planned. Thick plastic covered the surfaces. It was taped all the way to the ceiling. As he stepped deeper into the bathroom, he saw a thick lining on the bottom of the tub. It looked like a bed of Kevlar. Three ballistic vests lay there, one after the other.

"So you're going to shoot your innocent high school friend in your bathtub? Is that it?"

"Yup," Avery said behind him.

Drake turned around and saw Avery holding a pillow in his left hand.

"This is to muffle the shot. The plastic will collect all the blood, and the Kevlar will stop the bullets before they ruin my bathtub or, worse, enter the apartment below."

"You've thought of everything, Avery. I'm impressed. But you're still missing one thing."

"What's that?"

"How are you going to tell the police where I am? You see, I called them, and they know I'm here. They think you've orchestrated this whole thing from the start. When they walk in here and see this setup, they can prove you're the killer, and there's proof of premeditation. That's first-degree murder."

"You're bluffing. It doesn't matter, anyway. The police are not on their way here, and even if they were, I wouldn't *not* kill you. Not after what you did to Anne. Now, get into the tub, or I will put you there."

Drake struggled to remember the name of the cop in charge of the investigation. Avery pushed him. He grabbed for the wall to keep himself standing up. When he had one foot in the tub, he remembered the name.

"Spencer Milton is on his way here. I asked him for fifteen minutes with you alone before they came in to question you themselves. You gotta listen to me. He's on his way." Drake turned to look at him over his shoulder. "I'm serious. Don't do this. You will regret it for the rest of your life."

The Hungarians had to be coming since they hadn't killed him, and Avery was about to. All he had left was to stall for time. He was seconds away from being killed.

"I already regret everything, but it's too late," Avery said. "Once I started with Monika, I couldn't stop."

Drake stood with one foot in the tub and one foot on the bathroom's tile floor, his hands on the walls.

"After Monika, I felt a hunger for rape. It was such a rush. To date, I don't know how many girls I've forced. Most of them were prostitutes. I'd pay for my hour and then give them extra if I hurt them too much. But there's been a few late-night strolls in the park. Nothing seems to satiate the urge. So Drake," Avery glared at him. "I'm ready to die. I've gone too far and hurt too many people. Anne was my chance at a normal life, and you took that away from me by raping her. You're the sick fuck, not me."

"Okay, I can see that even if I admit to hurting Anne, you won't let me go, right?"

"Right. Now lie down in the tub."

Drake turned away and placed his other foot in the bathtub, his face aimed at the wall. He calculated that Avery would step closer now that Drake was fully standing in the tub. He heard Avery's voice and guessed his exact location.

"Lie down."

Drake turned, appearing as if he would lie down.

Then he spun, dropped low, and dove at Avery.

The gun went off.

Chapter 7

THE GUN THAT FIRED wasn't Avery's.

The bald guy with the snake tattoo, Laszlo, stood just inside the bathroom door, his brother slightly behind him. Avery lay on the bathroom floor screaming in pain, his right wrist bleeding from the new hole in it. Drake lay on the floor by the cupboards.

"Get up," Snake Head yelled.

Drake got to his knees slowly, then stood. He took a scan of his body but saw no blood. A smile crossed Laszlo's lips.

"Your new look. I like it. There's something to be said about being bald." He offered Drake the gun. "Take this. After what he did to Monika all those years before, you kill him."

Drake shook his head, unsure if his voice would work yet.

Laszlo lunged with a quick jab to Drake's face. It was

lightning quick and hurt like a son of a bitch.

Drake leaned over the bathroom sink, a hand on his cheek.

"I said, *take this*. We heard you say in the living room that you would've killed him. So do it."

Drake took the gun. He didn't want another punch in the head.

"How long were you here?" Drake asked. "He could've shot me. Why'd you wait so long?"

Avery rolled on the floor, his screaming reduced to moans.

"We don't answer to you. No more questions. Just kill this piece of garbage."

"Then tell me how you got into the apartment without making any noise."

Snake Head turned back to his brother. Attila nodded slightly. Snake Head looked back at Drake. "The superintendent has a set of master keys for all the apartments. We asked him politely. Or should I say, we removed the keys from his body when he refused. You just have to think. You can do anything if you plan it well and think. The best thinkers win all battles. That's why you're losing this one. You're not thinking."

What the fuck? Drake thought. *Murderer turned Tony Robbins.*

"Now, turn and fire that weapon into your old friend for what he did to Monika."

Drake lifted the weapon. A button on the side looked like the safety.

"Is the safety off? I assume it is as you just used this weapon to shoot him."

"Yes, the safety is off. Go ahead and finish this."

Drake turned toward Avery. The wild-eyed look of his old friend, who now knew some of the truths Drake had tried to explain, had pissed in his shorts. Urine pooled around his buttocks.

"Did you picture this was how you were going to die after all the horrible things you've done? How could you, Avery? I was your best friend." Drake worked himself up. He needed to for what he had planned. It was time to start *thinking*. He would take Baldy's advice and think his way out of this.

"This is for all the girls you've raped." Drake spun and fired the weapon about seven inches from Laszlo's face.

It was too close to miss, yet Baldy didn't budge. The weapon had only made a clicking sound.

"See what I mean?" Snake Head said. "You don't think, Drake. Would I seriously hand you a loaded weapon? I had one bullet in that gun, and it was intended for Avery. Handing you the gun was to see if you would shoot Avery. The man who took away your life and all the happiness you could've had? Would you shoot this man who took part in ruining Monika's life, too?" Baldy shook his head. "No, you wouldn't. You didn't think, and you don't have any balls."

He held out his hand. Drake handed him the weapon as he leaned against the bathroom counter, spent.

"Now, step out of the bathroom so I can finish this."

"Is there another way?" Drake asked.

"Avery and Kory chose this way long ago, so no, there is no other way."

Drake eased by Snake Head and stood at the door.

"Stay and watch, or the same happens to you," Snake

Head warned.

Attila had a gun in his hand. He crowded Drake near the door and whispered, "Don't move."

Laszlo lifted Avery onto the edge of the tub. The sound of plastic crinkled under their feet.

"Do you have anything to say before the end?" Baldy asked.

"Fuck you," Avery spat out. "This has all been some kinda joke, right? If Drake wanted to kill me and have it look like you two did it, then he would've already. Now I know he doesn't have it in him. See, I'm figuring it out. This was just about rape. I know how people like that think. Drake raped my girlfriend, and now he wants to rough me up. Okay, I get it. Now it's over." He looked down at his wrist. "Get me something to wrap this bitch. It's bleeding like a whore."

It sounded like the death rant of a delusional man.

Baldy produced a foot-long knife from inside his jacket and moved his arm back and forth twice.

Avery screamed and fell backward into the tub. Blood shot up from Avery and splattered on parts of the plastic. Baldy turned and motioned for Drake to step in and get a closer look. The brother pushed him from behind, causing Drake to stumble forward.

Avery lay in the tub on his back, his breath coming and going like he'd run a triathlon. His good left hand was over his crotch. All Drake could gather was that Baldy had used the knife to slice across Avery's groin. He saw a few pieces of bloody flesh sticking out of the new hole in Avery's shorts. The best way to heal rapists of their compulsions was castration. Drake felt no sympathy for Avery. He stepped back, nodded at Baldy, and walked out to stand by Attila.

"You've seen all you need to see here," Laszlo said. He turned back to Avery, who was still moaning. "Don't worry," Drake heard Baldy tell Avery. "It won't take long." He turned back to Drake. "This is almost done. If you think you might have a chance, you don't. You're fucked with what we have planned for you. There's nowhere you can run. Nothing you can do. Leave now, and good luck out there. We'll be watching."

Dazed, Drake felt Attila's hands on his shoulder. He pushed him toward the bedroom door. Drake reached the door and had his hand on the knob when he realized he forgot his camera in between the sofa's seat cushions. He opened the door and slammed it shut. The brothers would think they were alone. He tip-toed to the couch and retrieved his camera. Outside, the apartment's balcony angled down past the living room.

He touched the sliding door as Avery shouted something inside the bathroom. It was a piercing scream of pain that sent chills through Drake. He opened the sliding door fast, using Avery's scream to cover the sound. Then he hopped out onto the balcony and walked to the end. A separate door led to the balcony from the master bedroom, as he had hoped.

The curtains were open enough for the lens to peek through, but the room was too dark. Not enough light came from the bathroom. He would need to use the flash.

Drake angled the camera and waited for the brothers to reveal themselves. He didn't have to wait long. Baldy stepped to the doorway, wiping his hands on a towel. The towel turned red.

Attila moved out of the bathroom and into the bedroom to get out of his brother's way.

Drake pressed the button to take the picture. The flash shot at the same time. Then he turned quickly and ducked away from the window.

In seconds, either brother would be at the sliding door. He edged down to the open living room door, waited, and listened. The curtains moved in the bedroom. The lock clicked, and the door started sliding.

Drake hopped back into the living room and ran for the apartment door. He opened it and ran down the hallway and into the stairwell door before he heard anything behind him.

He had made it out.

As fast as his weak legs would take him, he jumped down each floor and then ran out the back of the building, through the parking lot, and across to the street behind High Street, leaving his old friend to die in a bathtub.

At the next corner, he slowed, caught his breath, and looked behind him.

Neither brother followed.

He flipped the camera around and turned it on to see the kind of picture he got. It was a side profile of Attila and a darkened silhouette of Laszlo.

Perfect.

Now, he would contact the police, talk to Spencer Milton, and give him the photos of the two men who killed Avery Hammond. Maybe, just maybe, Spencer would listen to him when this was all over.

He crossed the street and walked until he saw a Tim Horton's coffee shop on the right. He ran in to grab a large black coffee.

Think. He had to think. There was a way out of this. He just didn't know how yet, but he knew there had to be one.

He walked north on Hurontario Street, sipping his coffee, thinking.

The first step was to get to a pay phone and call Spencer. It would be a start. It would appear that he was willing to work with the police.

The second step would be to learn more about Monika Szabo. He needed to find out what happened to her in more detail and reread the newspapers from twelve years ago. Maybe research her family name. Was there any kind of immigration record or a way he could find out if Monika were in the country? Or was it just her brothers here terrorizing him?

But where could he do that kind of research? His apartment was compromised. His parents' place was out of the question. He had a couple of friends, but none of them would shelter him as aiding and abetting was a serious crime when the known criminal is currently invoking a *fucking* manhunt.

The library.

He would go to the library and use one of their computers to scour the internet. Or he would see if there was anything on microfiche or whatever libraries use nowadays.

It just so happened the Mississauga library was a twenty-minute walk north off Hurontario on Burnhamthorpe Road.

He saw a pay phone across the street. He took the last swig of the coffee, discarded the cup, and grabbed the two quarters the phone would cost out of his pocket.

After a two-minute search, the vandalized phonebook gave him the telephone number of the police department in Toronto that he would need to call.

It rang three times before someone answered.

"Toronto Police. How can I direct your call?"

"Detective Spencer Milton, please."

"I'm sorry, but he's out on business."

Drake put it more succinctly. "*I'm* his business. My name is Drake Bellamy."

"Hold, please."

He waited, tapping his fingers, watching the traffic zip by the phone booth.

The line clicked, and a woman picked up. "We've had seventeen calls today alone with tips on Drake Bellamy's whereabouts, three of which said they were Drake himself. How do we know it's really you?"

Drake double-checked his surroundings to make sure no one was watching him. He wondered how long it would take for them to trace the call. Maybe they were already on their way. Maybe he should have used his cell phone or a disposable one.

He needed to *think*. He needed to start *thinking* more, or he wouldn't be able to stay on top of this.

"In an apartment building on High Street, apartment 404, you will find the body of Avery Hammond. It will be another body connected to me. I have proof that I didn't kill him. I have a picture in my camera of the murderers. Tell Spencer I will email him the photo. I *will* call back, and I *will* be connected to Spencer Milton directly, or it will be the last time I call."

Drake hung up the phone before she responded. He shuffled off and ran across the street. Going north on Hurontario again, he relaxed as he detected no one following him.

Before entering the library, he entered Square One

Shopping Center and bought a disposable cell phone. Once he prepaid for an allotment of time, he headed for the west door of the mall.

Outside and across the parking lot, he dialed the police station's number from memory. He gave himself five minutes to talk as that would be how long it would take to get to the library, and he needed to keep moving.

It was answered on the second ring.

"Toronto Police. How can I direct your call?"

"Put me through to Spencer Milton."

He heard a click and the distinctive background noise sound as Spencer was on a cell phone, too.

"Spencer here."

"This is Drake Bellamy."

"What can I do for you?"

So nonchalant. What was his game? Whatever it was, Drake didn't find it amusing as his life was basically over, and he needed the help of the police. He didn't need attitude.

"I'll repeat myself. I am Drake Bellamy. I'm the guy you're looking for. I have information about the men who are murdering people."

"If you have information, then give it to me?"

"I just got it at great personal risk."

"You want my sympathy?" He cleared his throat. "Was it you who called in twenty minutes ago saying you have a photo of the alleged killers?"

"Yes. I took the photo on Avery Hammond's balcony. It's a good shot of the two men who have been terrorizing me and my family for over twenty-four hours."

"I'm on my way to Avery's apartment. You're saying that I will find a body there?"

"Yes. Avery's."

"Who is Avery Hammond? How's he connected? And where are you? Why don't you come on in, and we'll talk? Maybe we can figure this whole thing out before it's too late."

"It is too late. I will solve this on my own. In the meantime, give me an email address where I can send you the photo from my camera."

Spencer recited an email, and Drake committed it to memory as he walked closer to Mississauga City Center.

"I didn't do what you think I did," Drake said. "I didn't hurt anyone. I was simply going to buy medical weed for my mother, as she is dying of cancer. When I got to the apartment on Victoria Park, they had already killed Anne Keeley and left me to take the rap. The girl in my apartment was planted, and even though it will look like I killed Avery when you get there, I didn't. I'm clean and innocent, and one day you will believe me."

"I do believe you. Just tell me where you are so I can pick you up for a drink. We'll talk about everything and solve this together over a latte."

Drake thought about it. It would be easier. The pressure of the police would be gone. He wouldn't have to worry about the brothers as he would be in police custody, and when they killed again, Drake would have the perfect alibi. Maybe this was over. Maybe he should relent and tell Spencer where he was.

"No, I've got something to figure out first. Something about this whole mess doesn't make sense. Monika wouldn't do this to me. She loved me as much as I loved her. There's something else to this, and I'm going to figure it out."

"Monika, who—"

Drake snapped the phone shut and entered the lobby of the Mississauga library. At the desk, he was directed to the computers and set up with a code to access the internet. In minutes, he was online, looking back to the night when Monika Szabo disappeared.

After ten minutes of searching, he only found a small article in the *Toronto Sun* saying that Monika was missing. There was nothing else.

It took twenty-five minutes to find another piece on Monika. It stated how she had shown up four months later in Budapest, Hungary. That was about the time the police had stopped harassing Drake regarding her whereabouts. Once she had been located, the missing persons report was filed as found, and the case was closed. The newspapers had nothing else.

Drake took a moment to scan his surroundings. No one paid him any attention. A few people stood in aisles, and others sat at the computer banks, but no one seemed interested in him.

He looked back at the computer and did a Google search of the last name Szabo. Thousands showed up. Apparently, that was quite a popular name in Hungary.

"Shit."

When he lifted his head, two men on other computers were looking at him. He dropped his head to avoid their stares. Since the media had broadcasted his face everywhere, the risk of someone recognizing him was high, even with the shaved pate.

A quick search of the Princess Margaret Cancer Hospital in downtown Toronto gave him their address and phone number in case he wanted to visit Kory before he died. He also checked out Hepatitis C and how it is treated. Better to know a little about the disease in case he needed to talk his way through the hospital.

Five minutes later, he was done with the internet. His search on immigration websites for whether or not any person named Szabo had recently entered Canada was fruitless. Too many privacy issues with it. There was no way he could find out if Monika was in Canada or not. As far as the world knew, there was no rape on that fateful night twelve years ago.

When he glanced up, a woman sat staring at him five tables over. Before averting his eyes, he stared back. Something about her made him look again. Was it the scars on her face? She looked like she'd fought with a bear. Was it the intensity of her eyes?

After a moment, Drake figured it out.

It was because he recognized those eyes. He had stared into them many times before.

Those eyes belonged to Monika Szabo.

Chapter 8

Drake logged off the computer and rose from the table.

Monika rose, too. She turned from him and started for the side doors.

Drake moved quickly but not quickly enough as a couple of slow-moving students got in his way. He uttered an *excuse me* and rushed past them. Twenty feet behind, Monika as she exited the side door and turned to the right.

Drake broke into a sprint. He hit the door running and went outside just in time to see Monika turn the corner toward the parking lot.

"Hey!" he yelled after her and continued running.

At the corner, he lost her. She was completely gone. Either a car had sat waiting for her, or she slipped back into the building.

He started across the parking lot. He would walk through Square One Shopping Center and make his way to the buses that would take him downtown.

There was nowhere else to go. He had no leads left. Everything led back to Kory. He was the only one left who had participated in the heinous crime of that night twelve years ago. Maybe he would be able to offer some clue as to Drake's next move. Or maybe it would all be over with Kory's death. Would it end there? After Kory dies, will there be any more killing?

He thought about Monika. How did she know where he was? How could she track him so well? Did she follow him all the way from Avery's apartment? If so, could she have been close enough to hear his conversation with Spencer Milton?

Drake thought he must look paranoid as he didn't go more than four steps without turning to check behind him.

Monika and her brothers were professional trackers to have been on his tail so well. They must have him down to a psychological profile to know his every move.

That meant they would expect him to go see Kory. And then they would show up and kill Kory and make it somehow look like it was Drake's doing.

No—not this time. He would *think*. He would beat them at this. It wasn't about saving Kory's life. He was already dying, and after what Drake heard Kory had done, the guy deserved to die. Drake just had to talk to Kory and leave the building before the brothers got there. Or if they were there already, he would have to figure out a way to do it without their knowledge.

Drake was almost at the south entrance to the mall when he checked behind him again.

He was being followed by the brothers Szabo. That was

how they did it. They kept Drake in their sights, never letting him go. That was how they always just showed up. But with Drake entering a mall, he could be lost to view. Drake could scatter and leave through any mall entrance, thereby disappearing.

That was why they remained so close. They didn't want to lose a visual of him.

He looked back again and saw the brothers walking faster, attempting to close the distance before he entered the mall.

Drake rushed up, opened the mall's door, turned to them, waved, and disappeared inside. He walked away from the doors, past the Army and Navy store, past the center kiosks, and into the main part of the mall. A backward glance confirmed the brothers were close. They kept their distance now that they had him in sight again.

In order for Drake to get downtown and see Kory, he had to shake the tail. He would take Snake Head's advice and *think*.

Think, dammit, think.

Then he remembered an important fact about Square One and continued toward the large department store at one end.

Finally, he was thinking. His plan would shake his tail for sure. The brothers were going to be super pissed about it, but after what they had done to him, a little payback felt great.

One last look, and he saw both of them twenty feet behind, smiling as if the mouse was caught in their trap.

If only they knew they were the mouse now.

He turned into a store and was lost from sight. He waited for a count of three seconds, then turned around and walked back out and directly into the doorway of the Mall's little police station.

Square One had police officers on duty inside the mall. Their office was right beside the large department store's mall entrance, and as Drake entered it, both brothers walked by out front.

"Can I help you?"

Drake pointed out the window. "You see those two guys. They were stealing stuff at the music store."

The cop got to his feet and asked, "Are you sure? You saw them do that yourself?"

"Absolutely. The music store staff were too busy to notice. The guy with the snake tattoo saw me watching them. They followed me here. I'm scared. Can you help me?"

"Wait here," the cop said as he ripped the door open and turned in the direction the brothers had walked.

Drake watched him talk into a lapel mic.

He waited half a minute, opened the door, and left the office. He left Square One through a side door and started for the bus stop across the street.

He looked behind him as often as he could, but no one followed.

After a ten-minute wait, he was on the bus en route to a transfer and, ultimately, downtown.

He idly wondered what the brothers thought of him now. Would they be detained? Were they in Canada on legitimate papers? Did they have their passports on them?

Maybe luck would be on Drake's side, and the two Hungarian assholes would be out of commission for a week or more. He could only dream.

It was late in the afternoon. He had no idea what visiting

hours were at the hospital where Kory was being cared for. Drake fished out his disposable cell phone and dialed the number he had committed to memory from the website.

"Princess Margaret Hospital, how can I help you?"

"I'd like to speak to a patient. His name is Kory Adler. Could you put me through to his room?"

"Hold a moment while I look up his name."

The bus lurched on toward downtown Toronto. Drake waited a full minute before the woman came back on the phone.

"Kory is asleep at the moment. You'll have to call back."

"Is he still in room 417, or did they move him like they said they were going to? I thought I heard they may have a new liver for him."

"One sec … he's on the third floor. They must've moved him."

"Okay, I should be in before visiting hours are over. Thank you."

"Thank you," the woman said and hung up.

Perfect. He knew Kory was on the third floor. Now, he needed to get there, dress in scrubs, and convince a nurse that Kory was supposed to be moved.

Now he was *thinking*.

Fuck the Hungarians.

Chapter 9

DRAKE CHECKED THE TIME on his cell as he walked up College Street toward the hospital: 6:18 p.m.

No one followed him. He had shaken the tail. Monika and her brothers had no idea where he was unless they'd wired him somehow. They could suspect that he would go see Kory, but they had no idea he was there then.

Drake entered the hospital and took the elevator to the third floor. He walked the corridors as if he belonged there. No one took a second glance. Near the stairwell was a door that led to a janitor's closet. Inside, he found nothing that would help him. He left that room and dropped to the second floor.

At the bottom of the stairs was a changing room for doctors. He walked in and discovered lockers and showers. All the lockers appeared to be secure. It wasn't until he reached the shower area that he found a locker door sitting half open. The shower was running as if someone was coming on shift or leaving.

Drake scanned the contents of the locker and found what he needed.

After a quick change, he looked the part. The shower turned off. Drake ran for the exit and stepped out fast, almost bumping into a nurse pushing an empty stretcher.

"Oh, sorry," he muttered.

She angled around him, nodded, and continued down the corridor.

Drake headed for the stairwell. He walked to the nurses' station on the third floor and picked up a clipboard.

With the hospital coat of a doctor and the look of one, Drake felt confident he had the part sewn up tight.

A nurse walked over to the desk with files in her hand. Another nurse sat in a corner, studying the screen of a computer.

He nodded at the closest nurse. She nodded back.

"I'm waiting on the paperwork for Kory Adler."

The nurse looked at him, frowning. "Paperwork?"

Drake set the clipboard down. "Are you new here?"

"No," the nurse said. "I don't recognize you, though."

"I'm a specialist brought in to oversee the liver transplant of your patient, Kory Adler."

"I wasn't informed that a donor had been found."

"A donor was located in Vancouver. The liver will arrive within the hour. I'm here to talk to Kory and get him down for prep. When was the last time he was given any Ribavirin or any pegylated interferon drugs?"

Drake hoped beyond hope that his pronunciation was good enough to pass criticism.

"I have no idea. It will be on his chart."

Either this nurse did not know about the drugs Drake knew were being used for patients with Hepatitis C, or the words were pronounced correctly. He audibly breathed a long sigh. Then he took a deep breath and asked, "Which room is he in so I can review his chart before prepping?"

The nurse pointed down the hall. "Room 315."

"Thank you," Drake said, then walked around the nurses' station counter and headed to room 315.

He didn't knock when he got to the door. He opened it and entered like he owned the place. Then he strode right up to the foot of the bed of the rapist and grabbed his chart.

Drake was a forklift operator. He lived a quiet life with Sunday dinners at his parents' house. This wasn't him. He'd never done anything like this before. Impersonating a doctor was beyond what he thought he would ever do, yet it felt so natural. He felt he was actually good at it. He felt the rush of hoodwinking people. It was a rush he was growing to enjoy.

He also noticed that, overall, people were pretty naïve. They worked tirelessly to avoid confrontation. The only ones who welcomed confrontation were the most afraid on the inside. With confidence and an air of witty repartee, Drake knew he could do well maneuvering around until everything was over and he was either dead, in prison, or a free man eating Sunday dinners with his parents again.

While glancing at the chart and not knowing what half of it said, Drake smiled to himself. No one knew who he was or where he was. The only lead the brothers could possibly have was Kory's room in 315. That needed to be remedied quickly. There were no more leads, and no one else was responsible for that terrible night twelve years ago. At least as far as

Drake remembered.

He looked at Kory, sleeping fitfully. The man had lost a lot of weight. Not that Drake could remember him well enough from their high school days. Just that the man before him was seriously thin. Kory wasn't hooked up to anything that would beep, which was a relief. Drake didn't have to worry about setting off alarms at the nurses' station.

He set the clipboard back on the hook at the end of the bed and walked around, securing the bars on the side so that Kory wouldn't fall out when Drake rolled the bed from the room.

Whether Kory lived or died, Drake didn't care. What he'd recently heard about Kory made him feel that the wisp of a man before him was an animal who deserved nothing better than a painful death. Anger brewed inside him, and suddenly, he wanted to use a pillow over Kory's face for what he did to Monika, but he needed answers first.

Drake pulled on the hospital room door and propped it open with the door stop that he flipped down into place. He got behind the bed, pushed it quietly out of the room, and angled toward the freight elevator on the right, away from the nurses' station.

"Oh, excuse me. You can't do that," he heard behind him.

Just watch me, he thought.

Over his shoulder, he said, "I received a page on my beeper to bring Mr. Adler to the second floor for prep. I'm sure the paperwork isn't far behind."

"But Doctor, that's not how it works here."

He could hear her running up behind him. He reached the elevator and pushed the button. It was already sitting on the third floor. The doors opened slowly. As soon as there was enough room between the doors, he shoved the sleeping Kory inside. No matter how confident he felt about getting Kory alone for at least five minutes, he still felt quite scared. His stomach was a mass of knots, and his legs wobbled.

The nurse was near the door now.

"Doctor?"

The doors started to close. Other feet were running in the hallway. More people were coming. The doors closed agonizingly slowly. The nurse's face appeared in the crack.

"But prep isn't on the second floor. Where are you taking the patient, Doctor?"

Her words were quieted by the door and then silenced as the elevator lurched up to the sixth floor. He looked down at Kory. How could this man have done what Avery said he did? How could it be? Where would Monika and Drake be today if Kory hadn't shown up that night? Maybe a house in the suburbs, a fine car, and possibly kids?

All erased by one man's act. One man's evil act. And now that man is dying of cancer.

He deserves to suffer.

The elevator slowed, and the doors opened on the sixth floor. No one waited for him, which probably meant the nurse was trying to track down information on the false transplant and where her paperwork was instead of calling security. Or it meant the reaction time of the hospital security was slow.

He wheeled Kory out of the elevator, headed across the hallway, and into the first room he saw. Once inside, there were three beds, one occupied. A lone female, at least seventy years of age, lay quietly reading a newspaper.

She looked over as Drake wheeled Kory's bed into a spot

between the two empty ones.

"Do I have a new neighbor?" the old lady asked.

"For a short while. Right now, he needs his exercise."

Drake turned away from the bed and grabbed a folded-up wheelchair in the corner. He pulled it apart and brought it close to the bed. After unlocking the sidebars, knowing his time was short, Drake reached under Kory's shoulders and yanked him toward the edge of the bed.

The sharp movement woke Kory from his sleep. He wondered if it was painkillers that had knocked out Kory and kept him under until now.

He moaned and tried to stop himself from falling. Drake pulled and forced Kory's upper body over and off the bed. For all Kory protested, it wasn't a battle as he dropped perfectly down and into the wheelchair. Drake was surprised at how light Kory had been as he ran around to the front and lifted Kory's legs to be supported on the steel steps under his feet.

"Hey, what are … you doing?" Kory asked between breaths. Breaths that seemed like quite a struggle.

"We found a liver for you. I'm taking you down for prep."

Drake looked sidelong at Kory. He wanted to avert his gaze, but he also wanted to look into the eyes of the man who raped and tried to murder his Monika. Another part of Drake wanted Kory to recognize him for who he was so he'd feel fear. Surely, the brothers were intent on visiting Kory today, too.

In that one look, Kory saw who Drake was.

"No, no, no!" Kory stammered. "Don't let this man take me anywhere. Help!"

"I'm your doctor. You are in my care. The paperwork is all signed, and the transplant will happen—"

"NOOO!" Kory shouted, now quite awake and able to use his full voice.

If Drake didn't get control of Kory soon, others would come running to the room to investigate the disturbance, and Drake would be contained like a flopping fish in a steel net.

The old woman moved to the far side of her bed.

"Listen, Mr. Kory Adler, every time we have surgery, you act like this—"

Drake was cut off for the second time in a row as an alarm began blazing throughout the hospital.

The nurse had figured it out and raised the alarm. There was no paperwork, and he wasn't a doctor. He had to work quickly as security would probably seal off the hospital.

Drake wheeled Kory out of the room, not caring how loud Kory was as the din from the alarm muffled his screams.

The freight elevator still worked. It wasn't a fire alarm after all, and hospital personnel still needed to maintain care of the critically ill.

The elevator doors opened, and two security officers came barreling out.

"You there," one of them shouted over the alarm. "We're looking for a doctor wheeling a man in a bed. He was last seen heading to this floor."

Drake heard the man clearly over the alarm. The other guard had moved away. Drake didn't understand how they didn't see or pay attention to Kory's attempts at being noticed. They must be used to or ignore the routine taunting of patients.

Drake put himself in front of Kory and pointed down the

hall. He yelled back. "I saw a doctor running down the corridor to the end room with a patient in a bed. The patient was yelling something indecipherable. It's the last room on the right."

"Thanks," the security officer said, and both men ran away.

Drake ushered the wheelchair onto the elevator and pushed the bottom button. They dropped over seven floors without interruption. People were programmed not to use elevators during an alarm. Also, security was probably directing everyone up and not down.

The doors opened on a floor made of concrete walls. After wheeling Kory out, a sign said the hospital morgue was just down the hall.

The alarm had grown quieter in the morgue.

As he wheeled Kory along the corridor, he leaned down and whispered, "This will be your new home soon. Before Avery died, he said you were in this hospital. Think of our meeting down here today as symbolic. Maybe it's even ironic."

Kory remained quiet. He had to be thinking Drake was going to kill him, yet he wasn't fidgeting or screaming.

Drake wheeled the chair until he found an unlocked door. Inside, he was welcomed by a wall of cardboard boxes that held hospital files. He closed and locked the door behind him.

He walked Kory to the corner of the room and turned the chair around. He grabbed a couple of boxes and dropped them near the wall in front of Kory's chair to sit on. Now able to talk eye to eye, Drake posed his first question.

"Why did you do it?"

"If you came here looking for answers, you will leave sadly disappointed."

Drake shook his head. "Somehow, I doubt that. We've got time, as everyone is scouring the hospital above looking for us. They will never guess we're in the locked filing room. We'll have plenty of time to reminisce. So tell me, why did you do it?"

"You didn't go to all this trouble to ask me why. You could've called me on the phone or visited me during visiting hours to ask that without the risk of prison. No, you have come to kill me as you did, Avery and our girlfriends. You're no better than us." Kory spat on the floor.

His face had taken on a nasty, jaundiced look.

Drake shook his head. "You have no idea what you're talking about. What if I were to tell you that just over twenty-four hours ago, I didn't even know what happened that night at the lake? Would you believe me if I told you that I didn't rape or kill anybody, regardless of what the news is reporting?"

Kory licked his lips, letting his tongue protrude a moment too long. "We figured it out when the cards were mailed to us. It had to be you."

"So why didn't you call the police then?"

"Because I was dying, and Avery said he would be ready for your visit. Our crimes could still get us in trouble with the law, so we decided to wait and see if it was a hoax. To see if you were man enough. We didn't remember that side of you. But then Anne and my Michelle were found raped and murdered, so we knew you'd escalated things. It was too late to call the cops. Anne and Michelle were already dead, and we didn't want to tell anyone that we had prior knowledge you were gunning for us. Avery suggested we wait. When you show up, he would take care of you and then tell the police that you tried to kill him. It was the best we had to work with." Kory dropped his head and fumbled with his hands. "But you're here instead of Avery, so I know his plan failed."

Drake leaned back against the wall behind him. The alarm in the hospital suddenly stopped its monotonous squeal, leaving behind a ringing in his ears.

"His plan failed because it wasn't me who came after you two." Drake stared at Kory. "You really have no idea what's happening here, do you?"

"Sure I do. You've come to kill me."

"You couldn't be further from the truth. I'd love to kill you for what you did, but I came to talk to you to get some answers. Also, I came to warn you."

Kory made a derisive sound with his mouth. "Warn me. Fuck you. I'm dying. There's nothing anyone can scare me with."

"Interesting point, but I think there is. You're playing that tough guy role from high school, but you're scared of dying just like everybody else. You're see-through, Kory. We were all just too young to get it when we were teenagers."

"Whatever, man. Believe what you want. I'm not the one who'll be up on first-degree murder charges."

"You're over thirty years old and dying. At what age does someone grow up? Are you for real?"

"As I said a minute ago, fuck you."

"I saw Monika today."

Kory stared at him. He appeared to shrink in his chair visibly. "That's impossible."

Drake shook his head. "Nope. In the flesh. What did you do to her face?"

"Nothing. I did nothing to that bitch. For all I know, you're wearing a wire."

"Do you actually think the police would announce all over the news they want to pick me up for murder while the whole time I'm working with them? I'm the one who had the alarm set off. Do you think the whole hospital is in on it, too? Just to get a confession from a dying man? Just tell me what happened, and I walk out of here."

"No idea what you're talking about."

Drake narrowed his eyes and sat forward. "I know what you did and how you pushed Monika off the cliff."

"Think what you want. If someone hurt that whore, then she deserved it. Even though she asked for it."

Drake had a sudden urge to pummel the dying man. Women *never* asked to be raped.

"You're not in the best shape to be talking like that to the man who was going to marry Monika."

"Fuck you and your whore. Marry the skank. Like I fucking care. Oh, wait, I'm a tough guy here. I better watch myself. This isn't high school anymore, asshole."

Drake had no idea where the self-control came from. He literally itched to lunge at Kory but remained seated.

"Explain how she asked for it. Humor me."

"See, that's the part you don't know about. Monika called and asked me to come and rough *you* up. She wanted to leave you and couldn't do it herself."

"Bullshit."

"Is it? You have no idea what was really going on that night, do you?"

"Apparently not. Why don't you enlighten me?"

"Like I would go out of my fucking way to offer you clarity or, as you put it, enlightenment. Call the fucking Buddha, leave the Kory alone."

"Why are you so miserable?" Drake went out on a limb. "Is it because you feel you deserve to die? For all the wrongs you've committed? Tell me, Kory," he leaned in closer, "how many women have you raped since Monika?"

Kory looked away. His jaundiced appearance reddened as something akin to anger took over his features.

"Maybe it was good you came to see me after all. No one knows what I've done. Maybe by telling you some of it, the weight can come off my soul before I ascend."

"There'll be no *ascending* for what you've done, I assure you. But tell me anyway. We haven't much time."

"I kept a log back at my apartment of every woman that I've hurt, beat up, and raped. At least twenty prostitutes over the last decade. With these girls, you pay them enough, and they'll let you do anything you want to them. Sometimes, I went too far, and a few were hospitalized for a week."

Surprise and shock traveled through Drake's consciousness like a mist of sadness. Kory spoke of his rapes like he was proud. How could this be? Were people really like this? Were there girls like he described, willing to be beaten up for a price? What kind of world was this?

"Here's the best part," Kory said, a wicked smile in his eyes. "The ones who didn't see it coming. They are all sweet and innocent, asking what I want for my hour, and then boom," he smacked his hands together. "I punch them in the face, jump on them, and I'm inside their bloody vagina in no time as they're still recovering from the initial blow. Sick stuff, eh?"

Drake didn't know what to say. He recalled the *Slut Walk* that just took place in Toronto. Another one was scheduled for Hamilton in early June and other North American cities after what that Toronto police officer said at York University in January. He said something about how women could avoid getting unwanted attention if they would just stop dressing like sluts. Organizers and protestors set up these *Slut Walks* to say how one decides to dress wasn't an open invitation to rape. Women weren't *asking* for it. He also learned that approximately ninety percent of all rapes weren't reported. Apparently, the way the police and the legal system handled victims and their cases was documented as one of the main reasons. So it was *easy* for Kory to rape numerous women and get away with it because they generally wouldn't report it.

Of course, someone like Kory would feel women were asking for it.

Drake guessed that the rougher Kory was, the less likelihood anyone would lay a complaint for fear he would return and do worse.

Kory cleared his throat. "You want to know what the best part is. No condom. This isn't consensual, non-violent sex. This is me getting what I want. No wonder I have Hepatitis C. I'm surprised I didn't get AIDS." He cleared his throat. "I got to spread my Hep C it to whoever I could. If I've got a death sentence, then they do, too. A woman gave it to me. I give it back to them. All of them. Don't you get it? One woman is infecting all these other women. It's not me. I did nothing wrong. I'm the victim here. So because I got fucked over, I'm making sure to take as many women down as I can."

Drake wasn't sure how much more of this maniacal thinking he could handle. "You done? Because if you don't shut up fast, I might kill you myself."

"Do it, asshole. I know that's why you're here. Fuck you and do it already."

"Tell me why Monika asked you to rough me up."

"I did."

"No, you didn't. You spewed on about how fucked in the head you are."

"She wanted to leave you."

"I don't believe that," Drake shouted.

"Believe what you want. It's the truth."

"Why? Why would she want to do that? It's been twelve years, but I still remember how I felt about her and how she felt about me. We were deeply in love."

"You think so, but you're wrong."

"No, I'm sure of that. We were in love. You wouldn't know."

"There was something wrong in Hungary. It was connected to you somehow. Her words were, and I still remember them, *on the pain of death*. She couldn't be with you. She would rather die first. She thought she could trust me. When I got there and pulled her out of the car, she hit me in the face. That took me by surprise. That wasn't part of the deal. She wanted to play rough. I'm down for that. I'd already been raping and beating up girls for about three years by then."

"So you decided to rape her."

"Not at first, but she had it coming. Then I pushed her off the cliff because she asked for that, too."

"How? She actually turned to you and said, *please kill me, Kory, because I don't want to live?*"

"*On pain of death* were her words. So, I caused pain and death. Simple as that."

A noise in the hallway alerted him to watch the door. The sound of footfalls rushed by, and then someone talking down the hall calmed him again.

Then Kory started screaming for help.

Drake bolted into action. He threw his hand over Kory's mouth to quiet him. It only caused Kory to moan louder.

Drake had to get proactive and fast, or he would be discovered in this dank room and taken to a different kind of dank room. One with bars on the door.

With all the anger Kory had ignited in him, Drake wrapped himself around Kory's head from behind, using his right hand to cover Kory's mouth and his left hand to hold Kory's nose. Having lost the ability to breathe momentarily, Kory's volume decreased enough that anyone outside the door couldn't detect any sound from inside.

He whispered in Kory's ear. "I will let go and give you a breath if you promise not to make any noise."

Kory jerked his head up and down. The jaundiced color of his cheeks had turned full red again.

Drake eased off on Kory's nose. He detected Kory taking in a large breath.

Then Kory shouted so loud it made Drake jump.

He covered Kory's nose again. He heard a man in the hall saying something about, *this way, I heard it down here.*

His stomach dropped. Was this it? Was it a mistake coming to the hospital?

He looked around frantically. The room was in the

hospital's basement, with no windows. The only way out was through the door he had entered by.

Kory struggled in his arms. Drake held tight but ensured his right hand wasn't pressed against Kory's mouth to avoid being bitten. The last thing he wanted was to escape the hospital only to die of Hep C—the same thing that was killing Kory.

Footsteps were at the door.

He stared at the knob. It turned slowly. The door was pushed against the bolt that kept it locked.

Drake's heart entered his throat.

Through the door, he heard, "It's locked. Must be the next room."

Kory had fallen silent, the fight gone out of him. Drake knew he hadn't given him a breath in almost a minute, but he couldn't risk it yet. He held onto Kory's face tighter.

Maybe now Kory understands how serious this is.

He eased off on Kory's nose after ten more seconds, waiting for any sign of loud moaning to clamp back down again. With the back of Kory's head against Drake's chest and his right hand still clamped over Kory's mouth, Drake couldn't tell that Kory wasn't holding his head up on his own anymore.

No sound came from the hallway.

Drake eased his hands away and let go of Kory completely. The rapist's head slumped to the side.

"Oh, no," Drake whispered. "I didn't."

He reached in and checked for a pulse under Kory's neck.

"Shit, I did."

Drake got up, wheeled the corpse into a far corner, and

ran for the door.

Kory had deserved to die. He was a monster who had ruined the lives of many people. How many had he killed? As far as Drake was concerned, he had done the world a favor.

He put his ear to the door. After hearing nothing, he fixed his doctor's coat, spun his head around, and shrugged a couple of times. He took several quick breaths, unlocked and opened the door, and walked into the hallway as if nothing had happened.

He closed the door and started away from the elevators, down the long corridor where he turned to the right and continued walking. Behind him, he heard several people running.

"In here," someone shouted.

They must've found the filing room and Kory's body.

Drake picked up his step. Along the hall, he passed a door labeled *morgue*, and at the end, he found an exit door that appeared to be alarmed.

"Damn." He smacked his hand into the palm of the other.

Footfalls were coming to the corner.

He was trapped. Door number one or door number two?

He grabbed the door to the morgue, opened it, and ran inside.

The smell overwhelmed him immediately. He gagged and held his nose.

How the hell does anyone get used to this?

Hospital beds on wheels were lined up on either side of the small hall that led into the morgue. Each stretcher had a dead body on it, with a white blanket covering the body.

Two rooms were opening up on the right. Light from those rooms washed out into the dim hallway. In the second room, he heard the soft clangs and rattles of someone working.

He peeked into the first room. Large square silver doors covered one wall. The cooler. Cold metal tables lay in the middle of the room.

Drake figured it out rather quickly. The bodies were stored in the wall of each room. The stretchers lining the hall were waiting to be processed and stuck in the wall.

He needed to get on a stretcher. He needed to get covered by a white sheet.

Without missing a beat and knowing that this area would be searched after they found Kory's body, Drake looked for an empty stretcher.

There were none. He was out of time, and there was nowhere to go.

He knew there was no way he was going to climb up and lie down beside some deceased, decaying thing. He had to get under cover within a minute or sooner.

He would never last inside the cooler as he couldn't tell what temperature they kept those things set at.

A stretcher was the only way.

He had scoured the area and counted over twenty stretchers in seconds, but they were all full. Behind the second door, he heard someone making the subtle noises of what he thought was an autopsy.

He walked into the first room, dragging a stretcher with him as quietly as he could. At the metal table, he lifted back the white blanket to reveal a dead man in his mid-sixties. Luckily for Drake, he was in a cancer hospital. The man's body was emaciated to at least eighty pounds.

Drake had no choice. He had respect for the dead, but he

had more respect for the living. This guy's journey here was over. Drake's was still in full stride.

He steeled himself to lift the rigid body off the stretcher and onto the cold table, the whole time doing his best not to gag or throw up.

He could just see the headlines now: *Murder suspect found in hospital morgue because his stomach gave him away.*

Before jumping onto the stretcher, he needed to place it in succession so he wouldn't be the next one they tried to autopsy.

With the care of a newborn, Drake eased the empty stretcher out of the first room and walked slowly down the hall toward the second room.

At the edge, he peered around the corner to another sight that almost caused him to toss his cookies.

A female body, looking less than pretty, had a Y incision on her chest as a man in full scrubs worked on her. He mumbled unintelligible words into some kind of recorder that hung from the ceiling. Another pathologist stood off to the side near a bank of sinks, washing his hands.

Drake took a chance, hopped past the door, and ran down the remainder of the hall where the beginning of the line was for the incoming stretchers.

When he got there, he realized that the dead guy's juices would be all over the stretcher. He would love to have taken the time to clean it, but he couldn't, as there was no time.

He flipped the white blanket over so the part that touched him would be the clean top.

Asking God to allow this to work and begging Him not to allow his stomach to convulse, Drake climbed up and lay down on the stretcher on his back. A wet, squishy sound welcomed him as he nestled into place on top of the congealed goo from the dead guy. He adjusted the doctor's coat he wore so that most of the previous occupant's juices wouldn't touch him. He wondered how long this smell would stay with him after he left the place.

Knowing he was almost out of time, he lifted and adjusted the white blanket to cover his face to make it look as real as possible.

The door to the morgue opened down the hall. The same one that he had entered minutes before.

He held his head rigid and concentrated on his breathing as he heard men rushing into the morgue.

"Hello?" He assumed it was one of the pathologists from the second room. "Can I help you?" The voice was closer now.

"We're looking for a man dressed as a doctor. There's been an incident. Has anyone come in here?"

"No, it's just Robby and me. It's dead quiet down here." There was a pause. Drake figured the pathologist was smiling. "We would've heard someone running around if they'd come in. Besides, a man dressed as a doctor won't be hard to find in this place—it's a hospital."

There was another silence. All Drake heard was his own pulse beating in his ear.

"We're going to look around if you don't mind."

"Be my guest."

Drake heard footsteps. He heard the distinctive sound of blankets being moved and stretchers being bumped into.

At any second, his blanket would be yanked off his face. If it weren't his stomach that would give him away, it would be his nerves. It took great concentration to focus on calming the shaking in his hands. He tried thinking of better days, nice walks in the forest. He imagined he was lying on the beach, and the bumps under his back were small pebbles and not the juices of some dead guy.

It didn't work.

He thought about how righteous he was. Even though he'd actually killed someone, he was still the good guy. So, in the end, he had nothing to worry about. Even if they caught him here, he would walk away from all this in time.

Someone was close. It was maddening. He couldn't move. He had to focus on breathing to ensure his chest didn't rise too high.

He started counting his breaths. He remembered reading about certain forms of meditation and how they count each breath before going into a meditative state.

He breathed in slowly and counted one. On the exhale, he counted two.

His last memory was number seven.

Chapter 10

DRAKE JERKED AWAKE TO a vision of white. He pulled on it, and the blanket moved down and out of the way. He was still in the morgue. The lights above him were dimmed. As far as he could tell, the morgue was deserted as silence surrounded him.

He eased off the bed/stretcher. The sound of dried and crusted dead guy juice crackled as he moved, causing his empty stomach to roll. He hopped off the bed and hit the floor, then moved away from the stretcher and shook his arms and legs as if that movement alone could rid him of the smell and wetness clinging to his back.

The emergency exit lights illuminated the hall. He pulled out his cell phone and saw it was almost six in the morning.

Drake tiptoed to the morgue's main door and opened it slowly. The corridor was empty, the commotion from the previous night all but forgotten.

He adjusted his doctor's coat and rubbed a hand over his head. Stubble was already growing back. So much for the appearance change. Everyone knew what he looked like again.

He edged out into the hall and walked toward the elevator. As he waited for it to come down, he realized that things had changed with Kory's death. He had killed Kory. He had killed another human being. A sense of dread oozed over his consciousness. He could actually be arrested for a crime.

Drake Bellamy—a murderer.

He wasn't a murderer by nature. He didn't want to hurt anyone. He didn't ask for this. Yet people like Kory—after what he had done—shouldn't be allowed to live.

Even if women found the courage to lay a complaint, what next? Tell the investigating officers every detail? Then, live with it for a year awaiting trial, only to sit on a witness stand and testify to a group of strangers how she was violated? No, the only way to deal with people like Kory and Avery was either death or castration.

The elevator doors opened. Drake stepped into the empty lift and pushed the lobby button.

The doors shut, and he began to ascend.

He wouldn't let what he had done to Kory weigh on his conscience. A deep sadness clouded his mind at the thought of all the women Kory had hurt and infected with Hepatitis C.

Maybe that was why Monika was doing all of this. Could she have been handed a death sentence all those years ago only to return to kill those responsible and ruin Drake's life as he allowed hers to be ruined? He had tried to protect her all those years ago, but she must not see it that way.

The rules were changed in another way.

No longer would he be *their* victim. It was time to change the game on Monika and her brothers.

He also needed to know what Kory was talking about. Did Monika really ask him to come out that night? Why would she? And how did it have anything to do with Hungary? Drake had never been there, nor was his family from Europe. Whatever it was, it had nothing to do with him and everything to do with Monika.

The elevator slowed and stopped.

The doors opened to a quiet lobby. Drake stepped out and strode down a hallway to the right. He walked with the confidence and demeanor doctors often possessed.

A sign said the gift shop was to his left. In under a minute, after following the signs, Drake found himself standing in front of the little shop that was just opening their doors.

He hadn't looked yet but wondered how bad his back was. How much of the dead guy was still there, clinging to the rear of his lab coat? The smell remained in his nostrils, but that didn't necessarily mean people around him could smell it.

A woman in her sixties pulled the small bars that locked the front of the tiny shop aside and smiled at him.

"Long night, Doc?" she asked.

"Yeah. Pulled an all-nighter and slept like the dead in the locker room."

The woman curled her nose a little. "What's that smell?"

"Sorry. Haven't changed yet."

"I've seen worse."

"I'm sure you have," Drake said.

He needed to keep moving. If enthusiastic security or a police officer got a good look at him, it would be all over.

He walked up to the get-well-soon cards and grabbed an empty one where he could write the well-wishes in the middle. He asked for a pen and made the notes he came to make.

He paid for the card and a bottle of water and left the gift shop, avoiding any more small talk.

The main exit doors lay fifty feet away. He did not doubt that he could just walk straight out. The events of the previous night had simmered down. They probably thought the guy who murdered Kory had got away.

He hit the doors without incident and stepped into the morning sun. Birds sang as a light breeze cooled the air around him, dispelling the smell of the dead for the first time since he had entered the morgue last night.

He stepped down the main steps and started toward University Avenue. The brothers wouldn't be too far behind. They showed up at uncanny times. They were always there.

That meant only one thing: a tracking device of some kind.

Somehow, they had planted a bug on him.

Drake took a long swig from the bottle of water. A block from the hospital, he removed the doctor's coat and tossed it into a trash can.

The morning sun beat hot on his bald head. He took another drink and continued walking. The brothers would show themselves at any moment. He was sure of it.

Thirty seconds later, he saw them in a parking lot half a block down, leaning against the pickup truck Drake had seen the bald guy with the first day they had met on Victoria Park. It was only two days ago, but it felt like a week.

He continued walking as if he was going to avoid them.

Out of the corner of his eye he saw them talking to each other, watching him.

When he was even with them, Drake started across the parking lot toward them. Both men pushed off the pickup and stood with their arms crossed, heads tilted slightly back.

As Drake drew closer, Snake Head brought his hand around and placed it on the butt of a weapon that was hidden in his jeans.

Drake continued forward, only ten meters separating them.

Attila began clapping his hands. "Good job, Drake. Thank you for handling Kory for us. And tell us, how'd you escape?"

Drake stopped directly in front of them. Laszlo lifted his gun out and held it free at his side.

"You know you'll burn for that," Laszlo said. "Killing someone means you get a free ticket to Hell."

"There is no Hell. Earth is Hell enough. The things Kory did—that's Hell. I did the world a favor. I will do the world another favor when I kill you two."

The brothers exchanged a glance.

Snake Head said, "Big words for a dead man. We could've killed you time and again."

"Why didn't you? So I could suffer in jail? What is this, ruin my life like Monika's was? Take everything away from me and then let me rot in a prison cell? No, I don't think so. This has nothing to do with me and everything to do with you. Whatever happened that night, Monika asked for it. If she had wanted to break up with me, there were easier ways."

"Wow, you're learning a lot. But you still have no idea what's really going on."

"Tell me what happened to my parents."

"Nothing has *happened* to them. They're safe. This has nothing to do with them. I only needed your dad to call you with Anne's address on Victoria Park in Scarborough so you would show up that day. He refused, so he has a few bruises, but that's it. Very soon, this will all be over. You will either be dead, near death, or rotting in prison, and your parents will return home to live out their golden years, knowing their son was a rapist-murderer."

"How do I know my parents are okay?"

"You don't. Now fuck off."

Drake held up the get-well-soon card he had bought at the gift shop in the hospital so both men could see it. "Here."

"What's this? You're doing our trick with the cards? How imaginative."

"Follow the instructions, or you will both die, be near death, or rotting in prison by tomorrow. Deviate even a little, and I will also kill Monika." He gritted his teeth and spit the rest of the words out. "You will pay for what you've done. Be prepared."

He turned and walked away, his arms swaying with the energy that flowed through his veins. The hairs on his arms stood up. In his mind's eye, he saw himself going insane on both men, losing it on them. It would take no more than twenty seconds of constant flailing, and both would be on the ground writhing in pain.

The only thing stopping him was the gun still held in Snake Head's hand. One bullet in Drake's face and no fists would be flailing.

He walked a few blocks farther and turned into an alley behind the large Staples. The only place to have planted a wire would be his wallet. They couldn't risk him changing clothes.

In under a minute, he found what he was looking for. A small circular device was strategically taped under an inside flap of his leather wallet. It was a place where no credit cards or money would've been shoved.

Drake pulled it off the leather and pocketed the wallet again.

He stepped back out onto University Avenue and hailed a cab. As the driver neared, Drake got him to roll down his passenger-side window. When he leaned in to talk to the driver, he nonchalantly dropped the bug undetected inside the car, which fell between the passenger seat and the door.

"I need a ride to Thunder Bay. You going that way?"

"Thunder Bay?" The driver put his left arm on the top of the steering wheel and removed his sunglasses with his right. "You mean in northern Ontario?"

"Yeah."

"That's longer than a fifteen-hour ride, one way. You serious?"

"Absolutely." Drake smiled wide.

"Nope, not me." The cabbie pulled away, spinning Drake off the window.

He was in the clear. Monika and her thugs weren't anywhere to be seen. But, if they were following the bug, either of them could drive by where he was standing on the side of the road and realize their little tracking device had been discovered.

He hailed another cab in under a minute. When the driver slowed this time, Drake grabbed the back door handle and jumped in.

"I need you to take me straight to Prescott Avenue off of Keele and St. Clair," he said.

The driver nodded and hit the meter as he pulled away from the curb.

A block up, the driver did a U-turn, heading toward the Gardiner Expressway. Drake spun in his seat to see if he had a tail. He couldn't see the brothers' pickup anywhere.

He spun back around and saw the driver watching him in the mirror.

"I love Toronto," Drake said. "So many things to see, and I have so little time."

"Where are you from?" the driver asked in his East Indian accent.

"Kelowna, B.C. I've been here visiting a friend for the past week. I have to fly back tonight, and since this was my last day here, I thought I'd get a look around downtown again."

"It's not even eight in the morning. Downtown is just coming alive, and now you're leaving?"

"Yeah, well." Drake thought he was being quick on his feet. If somehow he was traced back to this cab, he wanted the driver to tell people that he would be at the airport tonight when he wouldn't. "I stayed down here last night and thought I would head back to my friend's place to spend the rest of the day with him."

The driver nodded. Drake turned to watch a building as they passed it and then looked behind him. No pickup. They hadn't seen him drop the bug. They had no visual. He had to be in the clear—at least, he hoped so.

Except for that cab. The one he asked if the guy would take him to Thunder Bay. It was right behind them, and he had a passenger. A female passenger. He could tell because of how the hair fell over her shoulders in the silhouette.

Drake sat forward and lowered himself in his seat.

They got close to Lake Shore Boulevard, and the driver turned right. Lake Shore Boulevard was almost empty heading out of downtown at this early hour. The cab sailed along, only stopping once for a red light.

Just after they passed the CNE grounds, Drake lifted up and turned around.

The cabbie with the female passenger was still behind them. He needed to find out if they were actually following him or if he was just being paranoid.

A story took shape in his head.

"Excuse me, Driver?"

"Yeah?" the driver said as he looked back at Drake in the mirror.

"I've got a small problem."

"You want me to pull over?"

"No, no. Not like that. A female problem."

"I'm not a therapist."

"I know, I know. I'm not asking you for help. I just think the girl from last night is following us."

The driver checked his mirrors.

"There's taxi behind us. How you know it's her?"

"I don't for sure, but it may be."

"Why she follow you?"

"She asked me to marry her last night. Said I was *the* one. Mister Right. She's an old high school fling. We met over drinks, and now that's it, I'm supposed to marry her."

The driver smiled. "What you say to her?"

"I was drinking and not too aware of my tongue and its betrayal. I said I would marry her and asked her to come to my room to discuss it further. This morning I just want to see my friend and go to the airport. She ran after me when I left the hotel, yelling that she would never let me go."

"Maybe she means it? If that her, then she's serious."

"That's what I'm afraid of. Listen, let's find out. When you turn north on Parkside Drive, take a left into High Park."

"Okay. Your dollar."

The taxi behind them stayed close. When the driver turned onto Parkside, Drake saw the driver check his mirrors. "They turned, too," he said.

"Okay, it's probably her. Turn into High Park and stay to the right. I will need you to pull over and keep the meter running. I'll get her to come out and talk to me."

"Whatever you want."

Drake stayed low in his seat. The driver turned left into the park. He then turned right and started up the little road that gave visitors access to the paths.

"Can you go faster?" Drake asked.

"It's posted at twenty kilometers here."

"Yeah, but you can go double that."

The cab sped up a little.

"Are they still behind us?"

"Yes."

"Turn left up there on that road. Park under the shadow of that tree and wait for me."

The driver nodded. "It's your dime."

Drake placed his hand on the cab's door.

"Hey, wait a second," the driver said as the cab started to slow. "How do I know you're not just going to run away?"

"I won't."

"No, not good. It happens too often. Give me some kind of deposit, or I'll call the police if you leave the car and walk away."

"There's no time," Drake said as the road was coming up.

"Deposit," the driver shouted, his right hand lying flat on the top of the seat in front of Drake's face.

He scrambled for his wallet. Inside, he only had a twenty and a five left.

"Will this do?" he asked, slapping the twenty into the driver's hand.

"Yes, this'll work, but the total fare will be higher."

"It's cool. I've got Visa. Now, pull over under that tree."

The driver jerked the wheel, and the cab came to a stop.

Drake jumped out and ran across the grass and back onto Centre Road, where he stood in the middle. The taxi that was following him was just pulling up. It slowed as the driver saw Drake.

The summer morning air had a glorious smell to it after spending so much time in the morgue. Yet he could still detect a subtle whiff of the dead in his nostrils. His heart rate beat at maximum capacity, and his stomach was more nervous than when he killed Kory.

The cab slowed to a complete stop. In the exact position it sat, the sun reflected off its roof, blinding Drake.

No one moved. No one got out of the cab. The driver just stared at him through the windshield. He didn't hit his horn.

Tension mounted as Drake waited. He barely noticed a

lone woman jogging by. The park was quiet while the two taxis idled.

Then, the driver in front of him dropped the cab into reverse and started backing up.

Drake ran. The cab lurched away faster. He wasn't going to let her get away. He ran harder, faster, then jumped. The driver had turned in his seat, looking behind him to steer better.

Drake landed on the hood and locked both hands inside the lip at the windshield, securing himself.

"Stop!" he shouted through the glass at the driver.

He saw the driver's face whip around and the surprise at seeing Drake so close.

The taxi slowed, and gravity moved Drake toward the windshield. When the cab stopped, it had veered off the road a little, the back tires resting on the grass.

Drake hopped off the hood, took two long strides, and ripped open the back door of the cab.

Monika held a gun in her hand, the barrel leveled at Drake's face. Up close, he saw all her facial scars. He remembered her beauty and was saddened at seeing her now. The pain she must have lived with, the undying sadness.

"Why are you doing this?" Drake asked, breathing through clenched teeth.

"You know why," Monika said. "You are to blame."

"I don't see that. How do you come to that conclusion? I was minding my own business two days ago. You started everything."

The driver's door opened. Drake could tell that the driver had seen the gun and was now running from the car.

"There's a lot of witnesses here," he said. "You really

want to be waving that thing around?"

"After hearing what you did to Kory, I wasn't sure who you were anymore."

"What? Are you fucking crazy?" he shouted. "After what *I* did? What about what you did to those innocent girls?"

"No one is innocent, Drake. Not even you."

"We're talking in circles." The police were probably being called. "Tell me what this is all about. Maybe we can talk. Figure out the problem without killing anyone else."

"You started this. I'm just ending it."

"Then tell me something. Enlighten me. When did I start it? How did I start it? Because I have no idea what you're talking about."

The gun wavered and shook. Her arm was weakening. Drake wondered if he could snatch it from her. Then she moved her right arm up and rested it on the back of the front seat, giving her a direct shot at his heart without holding her arm up anymore.

"In high school, you promised never to lie," Monika said.

"This is because of a lie?"

"You said you had no European heritage."

"I don't. I still don't. When I married you, I thought I would have some European heritage, but that didn't happen."

A tear formed in her eye.

"You lied to me, and that set a series of events into motion, and now I have lost my life because of it. So now you must lose yours."

"So you're going to shoot me? Is that it?"

"No. I want you to die like I am. I believe in fairness. Because of you, I was raped, beaten, and left for dead. My face had numerous surgeries, and I remained ugly. Now I'm dying because of that night. You will have the same fate. Your time is near."

"What the *fuck* are you talking about? Are you *even* serious?"

A vehicle was coming up behind them. Drake turned and saw the brothers in their pickup.

"Step aside, Drake, or I will kill you here and now," Monika shouted. "Do you want to die in High Park?"

Drake glanced back at her and whispered, "I loved you so much. You have no idea."

The tear he had seen in her eye a moment before dropped to her cheek. She quickly wiped it away.

Then she raised the weapon and said, "I warned you. I told you to step aside."

She fired her gun a foot from his face.

He jumped, closed his eyes, and flew backward at the sound of the weapon discharging at such close range. It was so deafening and shocking that he didn't register anything until he'd hit the ground and was sprawled out on his back.

Drake opened his eyes and was instantly blinded by the sun. He turned sideways and saw Monika jumping into the back of Laszlo's pickup. He leaned up on one elbow and examined his body for a bullet wound, finding none.

The pickup's engine roared to life, and the Hungarian trio sped away.

He shook his head and got to his feet. The two cab drivers were talking beside the cab he had arrived in.

The police were coming for sure now. He knew that. A weapon had been fired.

Drake lurched toward the taxi. His body was a mix of fear and adrenaline. He felt sludgy and sick.

"Can you still take me?" He heard his voice more inside his head than through his ears.

The drivers looked at each other.

"It wasn't my fault. I strongly urged her to leave me alone. But you know, some of those European chicks can be feisty." He looked between the drivers. "Look, tell him what the girl's fare was and add it to mine. I will pay for both. Just drive me up the street."

Drake didn't wait for an answer. He slid into the back seat of the cab and shut the door. The drivers mumbled to each other a moment longer, and then his driver got in behind the wheel.

He dropped it into gear and did a three-point turn, taking the road back out the way they had come.

Drake traveled north along Keele Street toward St. Clair and his final destination in minutes.

He checked the back window several times but saw no pickups or taxis following him.

Now, finally, the Hungarians couldn't follow him as they had no tracking abilities. He smiled as he realized that no one would know where he was for the first time in days. Only Mike would when he got to his place. And then he'd tell Mike what was happening and his plans. No doubt the police would be close behind after the cab drivers were talked to, so he couldn't stay long at Mike's place.

He knew Mike would come on board. He would only have a simple task to accomplish.

The Hungarian brothers were in for a treat.

He would have to live with how much he had loved Monika and how they had missed out on a life together.

But why? What had happened? And how had *he* lied?

He would find out tonight when the brothers did what he had written on the card.

They had no idea what a man in Drake's position would do or could be pushed to do.

They were about to find out.

Who's thinking now, assholes?

Chapter 11

THE CAB DROPPED HIM off a block from Mike's place. Now, the only question he couldn't answer was how long before the police arrived at Mike's place. Whatever happened, he couldn't be taken by the police yet. If possible, he needed to figure everything out first, then go to Spencer Milton with proof and a confession.

He knocked on Mike's door. No one answered.

He knocked again. It was early. Mike would have worked the night shift loading freight onto rigs. Drake had known Mike for three years, and in those three years working together at Pack N Ship, Mike had been an awesome boss. A friendship had formed, and now Drake would call on that friendship to see if he would help.

He knocked for the third time and then heard steps approaching the door.

A lock clicked. The door opened.

Mike stood there, his eyes bloodshot. "Whoa, do you ever look different? Nice shaved head." Then his face turned serious. "What do you want?"

"Your help."

"I'm not going to help you. That's abetting and shit. I knew something was wrong when you didn't show up for your shift, and I didn't get a call. Then I saw your name all over the news, saying you were wanted for sexual assault and murder. Are you fucking crazy? Why are you even here, on my doorstep? I couldn't get any work done yesterday as cops kept asking me questions like where you were and where your usual haunts were. Like, shit, man. It fucking sucks."

Mike wore only a pair of boxers. What Drake saw was a friend who felt he had been let down. Three years and Mike hadn't seen this side of him. And now, what Mike saw was a stranger.

"Mike, give me one minute. After that, you can kick me out."

Mike looked him up and down, then his gaze went over Drake's shoulder and scanned the street. After a moment, he stood aside and motioned Drake in.

"One minute. It's all you get. I don't want shit for this."

Drake didn't miss a beat. He started with Monika and how they were to be married. He finished by explaining why Anne, Michelle, Avery, and Kory were all dead now and that he was supposed to be their fall guy. He left out the part about how Kory died.

"Seriously, you're not shitting me?" Mike asked.

"Let me show you a picture."

Drake pulled out his camera and brought up the pic of the brothers in Avery's bathroom.

"Wow. Sick man. Truly sick."

"I need your help."

Drake described his plan for the brothers and what Mike's job would be.

Mike stepped away. He rubbed his eyes and looked back at Drake. "I don't want to get involved. These are bad dudes. As far as I understand it, you're only alive because they need a fall guy. They won't need me."

"With what I have planned, they won't even know you're there until it's too late. Even then, it'll be after midnight, and they won't see your face. Besides, it's where you work. You're expected to be there. Listen, Mike," Drake placed a hand on Mike's arm, "I really need you here. This is serious. If anything goes wrong, all you have to do is not move. Stay out of sight in the dark. Park at the back. No one will see you. Just don't move, and you were never a part of this."

Mike began pacing.

"Mike. We haven't got much time. The police are probably on their way here."

Mike's head snapped back up. "Here? Why?"

"Because the cab dropped me off here. They're going to figure out my boss lives on this street and think I'm looking for a place to shack up."

"The police won't act that fast."

"A gun was fired in High Park. Of course, they're going to be on this fast. I'm leaving. You should probably leave so you don't have to deny I was here because neither were you."

Mike stomped away and hit the stairs running.

"Hey, are you going to be there for me?" Drake shouted after him. "Will you show up tonight?"

"I have to go to work tonight, so yes, I'll be there."

Mike had reached the second floor.

"I mean, *are* you going to be there for me? Will you do what I've asked and help me nab these guys?"

More stomping and moving around upstairs.

"Mike? I need to know," Drake shouted.

"Yes. If everything you said is true, I have no choice but to help you." He yelled from upstairs. "I'm going to take you at your word. Now, get out of my house."

Drake ran through the kitchen. He exited the back door, ran across the wooden deck, onto the grass, and over the fence in the back. He ran through the neighbor's yard and kept running until he got to Keele Street.

On Keele, he used the last of his change to catch a bus heading south. He wanted to get as close to the lake as possible. On a late June day, the beaches would be busy with the sun shining as bright and hot as it was. The perfect spot to go for a little dip, rinse his body off, and then his clothes.

He would gather up his weapon to be ready for tonight's meeting.

He remembered an old quote about how the elevator to success was out of order. You'd have to take the stairs, one step at a time.

This was the first step. He had to clean up this mess. The mess that had become his life.

After that, he would have to deal with Monika.

He stared out the window of the bus, wondering if he would die later that night.

Chapter 12

After spending time at the beach, swimming in the lake, and rinsing his clothes, Drake couldn't smell the rotting scent of the dead from the morgue anymore.

He had slept under a large tree in a small park aptly named Budapest Park beside the busier Sunnyside Park.

Now, at ten thirty in the evening, his clothes were finally dry. He was well-rested and alert. He had gathered up his weapon but had no idea how the plan would unfold.

They couldn't track him anymore, and he had no idea where they had holed up. This was his only chance to deal with them. He had to succeed tonight, or things could get infinitely worse if that were possible.

He knew he should involve the authorities. He should let them know where the meeting was being held so they could swoop down and arrest the Hungarian brothers for what they had done. But that wouldn't happen. The police would show up and arrest him instead.

He walked toward his workplace by way of the rear of neighboring buildings.

He needed Mike. Without someone to operate the forklift and prepare the empty rigs to trap the Hungarian brothers, they could abscond with Drake or kill him, and it would all be over for Drake.

Fifteen minutes before the meet, Drake sat on a discarded tire behind a small bush in the rear parking lot of his workplace. He studied the building where he had spent years working late shifts driving his forklift. Some of the loading doors were open. Mike had done well, as there weren't a lot of skids sitting around the docks.

Three trucks were backed up to the doors. In door number three sat the only trailer without a truck attached to it. The others were a Mini-Max trailer heading to the Maritimes and a Transnat rig leaving for Quebec. He heard a single forklift maneuvering around the dock, loading the last of the skids for the night.

Pack N Ship sat at the end of Westside Drive off of The West Mall. There were plenty of options for escape. Drake knew this building inside and out. Along with Mike's help, knowing the terrain was another major reason for choosing this as a meeting place.

Because they couldn't track him anymore, Drake was sure they would show. There was no way they wouldn't.

He looked at his cell phone again: 11:57 p.m.

Where were they?

The docks were quiet now. He listened to the distant traffic on the Queensway. A lone car raced along The West Mall.

Drake waited. Inside the open loading doors, nothing moved. The forklift had entered a truck and stopped.

Something's wrong.

Mike should have a couple of guys still on shift. Or maybe he sent them home knowing what was happening tonight? The Hungarian brothers had explicit instructions. He had written it on the card he'd handed them at the hospital.

Or it could be that Mike had called the police, and everyone was waiting for Drake to appear.

He scanned the entire lot slowly and carefully, searching for movement. Anything out of the ordinary.

Nothing.

12:01 a.m.

What the fuck?

Cold steel rubbed gently against his left cheek.

He jumped and fell off the tire sideways.

"Get up. Do it slowly."

Snake Head stood above him, a long silver gun in his hand. Laszlo wore a Toronto police uniform.

"I said, get up. Look around you. No witnesses. I pop bullets into you right here, right now. Now, get up."

Drake had trouble getting to his feet. The worst were the nerves and how they betrayed him. His shaking limbs, flipping stomach, and rapid heartbeat all served him a platter of jellyfish for muscles.

He got to his feet without falling and stood facing Baldy on wobbly legs.

"Why are you wearing a police uniform?" he asked, then swallowed hard.

"Fuck you and start walking."

Drake started across the open gravel parking lot toward

the lighted building.

"What've you done with Mike?"

No one responded. He wondered if Snake Head was still behind him.

Then the asshole said his name, "Drake?"

"Yeah?"

"Turn around."

Drake stopped and turned to look at him. He didn't see the left hook coming, and even if he had, there was no chance to defend himself.

Baldy's fist connected with his right cheek, whipping Drake's head around. He almost lost his balance but stayed on his feet, bent at the waist.

A moan escaped him as his hands covered his cheek.

"Why'd you do that?" he managed to say through his half-closed mouth.

"No more questions. I should kill you for what you did."

Drake righted himself.

"Look." His mouth worked better as he had determined nothing was broken. His face felt swollen to double its size. "I have a question, but I'm afraid to ask it."

Baldy nodded. "All right, one question."

Drake stammered on his feet for a moment. "You said you should kill me for what I did. So what is this horrible thing I did? I mean, other than what you think happened twelve years ago."

"The fucking picture you took. I am very lucky that it only showed my brother's face. He's not known to the police. I wouldn't be here right now if it had been my face. Spencer Milton sent it to all our screens as soon as you emailed it to him. I came this close," he emphasized with his finger and thumb, "to buying a first-class ticket to prison with no get-out-of-jail-free card."

"That's old."

Baldy cocked his head sideways. "What's old?"

"That stupid monopoly cliché about get-out-of-jail-free cards. Everyone uses that. Pick something else."

Baldy shoved Drake hard enough to make him stumble.

"Shut the fuck up and get moving. You want humor? I will shoot you in the fucking crotch and then laugh. Watch yourself, Bellamy. Just watch yourself."

Drake stumbled toward the light at one of the loading doors. He dropped his hand away from his throbbing cheek.

Now he knew why he hadn't seen the brothers' pickup truck. An unmarked cruiser sat in the front of the building, hidden from the back where Drake had sat on the discarded tire.

"I don't believe you're a cop," Drake said. "No way. Not after what you've done."

"Smart," Laszlo said. "You didn't word that as a question. The truth is, I am a cop. And what have I done, exactly? You're the criminal here. You raped those girls and killed everyone."

"Yeah, and Santa Claus eats raspberries on a white pony while selling Peter Pan's dust to the Easter Bunny."

"No, you're just an asshole that killed a girl twelve years ago. Today, you get to spend the next twelve years dying, too."

So this was still about Monika and that fateful night. They were ten feet from the stairs that led into the building.

"I didn't call Kory or Avery that night. It was Monika who set everything up twelve years ago. She did this. I tried to save her and got knocked out for my effort. So whatever else happened that night had nothing to do with me."

"If you get a jury, you can tell them all about it. You can request one, as the crimes you'll be charged with are indictable offenses, which means you can choose a judge or jury. After tonight, it's up to you how you proceed if you make it."

Drake started up the stairs. The front door sat propped open.

When he stepped onto the loading dock, he saw why there weren't skids scattered throughout the warehouse. Someone had piled up all of them along the back wall. He turned in time to see both brothers enter behind him.

The look in Attila's eyes caused him to take a step back.

Baldy put a hand on his brother's chest. Their eyes met, and his brother stepped back.

"This was supposed to be easy." Snake Head looked at Drake. "But you fucked that up. Now, every police officer in Toronto and the surrounding area is looking for you and my brother. Because of you, he must leave town tonight when we're done here."

"We're done tonight?" Drake asked.

"Yes, this ends tonight."

A thought occurred to him. "Where's Mike?"

"In there," Snake Head said. He pointed to the trailer that didn't have a truck attached to it in loading door number three.

"Hey, Mike," Drake shouted. "You coming out?"

He felt his nerves were at their end. Mike was supposed to be here. The plan had been for him to work the silent electric forklift. He was going to wait until Drake met with the brothers, and then he would drive the forks under their vehicle and lift it off the ground. Then, he would leave the forklift without a key unattended. Drake would use his cell phone to call Spencer Milton, and the brothers would have to escape on foot, allowing the police a decent chance at picking them up with a good K-9 unit.

They also had a plan to use the trailer as a trap if it was needed. As soon as Drake had the brothers chasing him inside, Mike would drop the bay door, and Drake would escape through the door at the front of the trailer that Mike had already unlocked, securing it behind him. The brothers would be trapped inside the trailer.

But nothing of the sort was going to happen. The *police* were already here, and Mike had been found out. There was no pickup and no forklift to operate.

Drake moved enough to glance into the trailer where Laszlo had indicated his friend, his boss, would be. He detected the brothers moving with him.

The yellow end of a forklift came into view. Its engine was off, but the lights on the top of the forks were illuminated. Another step to the right, and Drake had seen enough.

He looked away and gagged. His stomach clenched, his throat locked, and then opened.

Not knowing if he could stand, Drake dropped to his knees. Snake Head was saying something about how serious they were.

"Did you hear me?"

Drake shook his head. He stayed down on his knees, holding his stomach.

Mike was impaled on the right fork. He had been tied to

a bar stool. Somehow, the bar stool and Mike were suspended at the end of the trailer on the wall. The fork went straight in through the middle of Mike's chest. The image that will be locked in Drake's mind will always be the one of Mike's head dangling down so far that it looked like he was trying to determine what was stuck in his chest.

Drake did this. By involving Mike, he had gotten him killed. Could he live with that? Should he live? Maybe he should stand up and attack these animals who paraded around in human skin. Nothing would slow him down. Not with the malevolence coursing through his veins at that moment.

Then, it would truly be over.

His breathing came in gasps. He felt red. He saw red. His tachometer sat comfortably in the red.

"I said, do you see how serious we are now?" Laszlo asked.

"Why? How?"

"I dropped my brother off at the end of the street to watch for you and to make sure you didn't make a hasty retreat. Then, I showed up in my uniform and identified myself to Mike. I told him that we had reason to believe a serial killer would be on the premises this evening. Either he helped us or would be arrested for aiding and abetting. It was simple, actually. He was more than happy to send the other employees home early. No one even saw me in the front offices. Then he told me all about your plans with the forklift."

Drake tried to compose himself. Laszlo was still holding the gun aimed at Drake.

Snake Head continued. "I got him to clear the floor, and then after we were all set, I pulled my gun, tied him to that chair, and hammered it onto a skid. Once he was placed on the back wall of the trailer, I had fun working the forklift into his chest cavity. He died over an hour ago, screaming and wailing like a stuck pig. He was *actually* going to help you. We can't have that."

Drake fought the urge to lunge. A crazy horned man sat on his right shoulder, screaming in his ear to murder the two men standing before him. A white angelic man sat on his left shoulder, shouting that the two men before him weren't human and, therefore, it wasn't a sin to hasten their retreat from this planet.

In Drake's head, a subtle shift took place. He would never be the same again. The shift in his head moved his emotions to a darker place and his reality to a knowing beyond that of right and wrong and into a realm that only dealt with justice.

At that moment, he became a new man. One that he would never have wished to be, but one that had been thrust upon him. He didn't resist it. There was a certain kind of power that came with the feeling. The power to kill these two men and enjoy it. They had raped and killed two girls that had nothing to do with what happened twelve years ago, and Drake was an official rapist-killer since he killed Kory.

"I'm a rapist-killer," Drake said. "I murder men who rape women."

Laszlo frowned. "What's that?"

"I said," he raised his voice. "I'm a rapist-killer. I killed Kory with these hands." He raised them to show the brothers. "And I will kill both of you with them. I assure you of that."

Snake Head stepped closer and brought his weapon up to an inch from Drake's nose. Drake didn't flinch like before.

He leaned into the tip of the gun and rested his nose against it, his eyes wide, breathing through his mouth. His stomach was settling, and his nerves were firing back in time. He felt as energized as if he'd been snorting Red Bull.

Baldy said, "You seek to test me?" He shook his head. "You don't want to test me."

"Fuck you," Drake said. It came out as if he breathed the words from his throat, deep and guttural.

"Why can't I shoot him in the face, Attila? Tell me again why I can't kill him right here, right now, and say we caught him murdering his boss, and then he pulled a gun on me? Spencer will be so happy to've nailed the bastard that he won't look too closely at all the details."

Attila touched Snake Head's shoulder and said, "Because we swore to Monika that we wouldn't kill family. This whole thing started because the family was dishonored. Killing him would only add to it, and we would be just as guilty. Father would never approve."

Drake pulled away from the tip of the weapon.

Family?

"What're you two talking about? Are you both fucking idiots? I'm not family. Monika and I never married."

Attila addressed him. "And it's a good thing you didn't. Monika would be dead, and so would you if you had. Nobody disrespects the family as badly as you two were about to. But she gets a free pass because she didn't know, and as soon as she tried to correct the situation, she almost died because of it. You and your friends took care of that. Now they're dead, and you'll pay for it."

"Just to be clear, I have zero idea what you're talking about. I was born here, in Canada, and my parents were, too."

"You keep telling yourself that. No problem. What do we care? You're fucked either way."

Snake Head waved the gun to the left. "Let's go."

He moved aside, expecting Drake to follow. After a moment, Baldy turned and told him to move again.

"How do you know I haven't called Spencer? How do you not know he isn't sitting outside right now listening to you two with some parabolic listening device?"

"Two reasons. One, you wouldn't let yourself get that close to being caught by the authorities, and two, I would've heard about it on my police radio. Now move."

Drake started walking. "Where're you taking me?" As he stepped forward, he waited for the right moment when Attila would be in the right place.

"You'll find out when you get there."

"Seriously, tell me, or we won't go anywhere."

Attila would be where he wanted him to be with three more steps.

"I'm afraid you don't have a choice," Laszlo said. "Monika is waiting for a reunion."

The time had come.

Drake reached into each pocket and grabbed a handful of the sand he had collected from the beach earlier in the day. He withdrew as much of it as he could.

In one fluid movement, he spun and threw the sand. It happened so fast that Laszlo could barely react.

It covered Laszlo's face in a cloud. His hands flew to his eyes as he screamed.

As soon as the sand had left Drake's hands, he dodged down and around Snake Head and then past Attila. Within a second, he already had a two-step lead on Attila.

Laszlo screamed as the gritty sand rolled under his eyelids. At first, his words were unintelligible. Then Drake caught the familiar lilt of Hungarian swear words.

By the time he had cleared the two men, the gun went off as Laszlo fired in Drake's general direction. He yelled for Attila to grab Drake.

The sound of the weapon was deafening. Even in the small warehouse with a few loading dock doors open, it rang true in his ears like Monika's had earlier in the day.

Without looking back, he knew Attila would be close.

"Stop him," Laszlo shouted.

There was nowhere to run or hide, as all the skids were piled in the back along the wall. The only place available was the empty trailer where his boss and friend Mike now sat impaled.

He turned for it. The gun fired behind him again. This time, the bullet was closer. The air cut directly in front of him, and a hole materialized inside the trailer door.

An inhuman wail came from Baldy as he knew Drake was still running.

Then Laszlo did what Drake had wanted him to do from the beginning. It was the only reason he had wanted Attila behind him. The gun fired in rapid succession, over and over. Drake dove for the cover of the trailer. Something hit the back of his leg while he was in the air. He landed hard on his shoulder and rolled into the wall. A frantic pat down informed him just how close a bullet had come to wounding him. There was a tear in the hamstring area of his jeans, but his flesh was untouched.

He looked up and into the eyes of Attila, who stood at the trailer's open door.

The man stood there for what seemed too long. Laszlo still wailed about his eyes from inside the building.

Blood formed on Attila's lips. He dropped to his knees, paused, and fell face-first to the trailer floor.

Laszlo had shot his brother Attila in the back.

Drake scrambled to his feet and ran for the front, where the forklift still held Mike.

"I'm coming for you, motherfucker!" Laszlo yelled from behind him.

When Drake got to the front of the trailer, he looked behind him. Snake Head stood over his brother's body. He snapped something into his weapon. More ammunition.

Drake was exposed with nowhere to go if Mike hadn't unlocked the side door like he had asked him to that morning.

Did he get to it before the brothers appeared? Drake would know soon enough—or he would be dead.

Snake Head raised his gun. "You are fair game now that you have killed my brother. I will not rest until you die for this."

Even though the logic was twisted because Drake hadn't actually killed Attila, he decided that now wasn't a good time to argue the point.

Drake pushed on the door.

The gun fired behind him.

The door opened.

Bullets hit the wood where Drake had been standing as he dropped to the ground outside. He stayed on his feet and ran.

He had one more thing to do. He ran around the building and came up to the front. He yanked the camera out of his back pocket, hoping it still worked.

The power button lit up.

He hit the night setting, lifted the flash, and took three pictures of Snake Head's police issue undercover vehicle.

Then he hopped the fence at the back of the property and ran down the small embankment to The West Mall, where he crossed the street and disappeared into the bushes on the other side, grateful he was still breathing.

Chapter 13

HE WOKE WITH A backache. The park bench he had spent the night on was rough and digging into his back. He got up and started walking, the loss of his friend on his mind. Head hung low, he tried to keep the tears at bay as he trudged toward downtown Toronto.

He had to learn if there was anything to the family tie-in issue the Hungarian brothers had talked about. He needed to do this while avoiding the authorities, and then he would take everything to Spencer Milton and let him sort it all out.

At least now, it was just Laszlo and Monika left. Once he emailed a picture of the police cruiser Laszlo had been driving, the police would put it together that it was Attila who was killed at the loading dock. Hopefully, Spencer would begin to see a pattern. Add that to the picture in Avery Hammond's bathroom, and either Spencer figured it all out, or he was an idiot.

There was no way he was connected to the Hungarians by blood. Maybe Monika only said that to break off their relationship. She told her brothers that was the case, and now they're working on that assumption.

Yet that couldn't be, either. It was too simple. They had to have a good reason for believing it, and not just Monika's word alone would be enough.

The only other people who might know the kind of information he was looking for would be his grandparents, who lived in Oshawa, about an hour outside downtown Toronto.

He walked until he reached Union Station. Once there, he sat on a bench and stretched, the morning sun warning him how hot the day would be.

He thought back to the previous evening. Why didn't they search for him when he arrived? Did they think he would show up without a weapon? What if he had carried a gun to the meeting at the loading dock?

He stood from the bench and stretched again. Police officers weren't all bad. He remembered an old friend from Barrie, a platoon leader in the Peel Region section of Toronto. He and his wife were both officers. Great people. They risked their lives numerous times in the line of duty. Always did the right thing. So, there's that.

A young couple walking a dog off the leash passed him. Another man in a suit was hustling as fast as his bulk would allow him to as he glanced at his watch a couple of times. Cars raced up and down the street, oblivious to the world that rotated under them. These people had families, jobs, and summer vacations to go on. Drake had no girlfriend, probably no job now that he got the boss murdered, and no place to live now that dead bodies had shown up in his bedroom. He didn't exist as a normal citizen of the city anymore. And yet here he was, about to go and find out about a past that probably didn't exist either.

One step in front of the other. Baby steps. That's how it will get solved.

He walked toward Union Station, stopped at a convenience store that was no bigger than a hole in the wall, and used his Visa to buy a baseball hat.

When he stepped outside again, he ripped off the tag and set the hat on his bald head. More stubble had grown in, matching his facial hair. Descriptions were out for the shaved head. The hat was all he had at the moment, so it would have to do.

He entered Union Station and mixed in with the thousands of morning foot traffic in downtown Toronto en route to a myriad of destinations.

He bought a ticket and went to the appointed platform. The GO train would take him to Whitby. Afterward, he would transfer to a GO bus, which would take him to downtown Oshawa.

He knew the route from there.

He snatched a copy of the *Toronto Sun*, the morning newspaper. While riding the train, he could use the newspaper to cover his face and get up to date on what the public was being told about him.

He got on the right train and sat in the back corner, waiting for the ride.

The front page of the news had a large picture of a Mormon Compound with the caption, *Hero Strikes Again.*

There's something, he thought. *I'm not front-page news*

anymore.

Some girl named Sarah Roberts had infiltrated a compound and saved a bunch of female kidnap victims. The paper was touting Sarah as a hero.

He read on. Apparently, this Sarah Roberts had been busy. The paper said it went back four years to when she was rumored to have saved a woman from a car accident off the Elizabeth St. Bridge.

Wow, that's some tough girl.

He stared at her face a moment longer, lingering on the curve of her cheeks, the soft-looking lips, and the long flow of hair. What stopped him was the intensity in her eyes. The cameraman caught her glaring at him. Her eyes told a story. *She's gorgeous but tough*, Drake thought.

He read the rest of the paper and was surprised to find nothing of the loading dock deaths from last night anywhere. Neither his boss, Mike, nor Attila made the morning paper. He set the paper aside as no one was paying particular attention to him.

It took four hours until he reached Cedar Street in south Oshawa. He turned right onto Dwight and began worrying as he approached his grandparents' home.

What if the police had talked to his grandparents? Could they be watching the house? Would they go to that kind of expense?

He decided to do a full walk around the entire neighborhood before committing to knocking on his grandparents' door.

He passed Kinmount Crescent and turned right onto Oxford Street. After a quick walk down Oxford, he turned right onto Kinmount Crescent again and started up the back way to his grandparents' house.

Nothing suspicious caught his attention.

He turned the corner in the middle of the crescent and slowed to stare at the front of his grandparents' house.

The front windows were open, which allowed a breeze to flow into the back-level split. Kids played in the street. A lone beat-up Vega cruised down the tight street between all the parked cars littering the area.

Nothing appeared amiss whatsoever.

Drake walked across their driveway, grabbed the front door, and pulled. It was unlocked. He stepped into the foyer and saw his grandmother at the kitchen sink doing what he assumed were the lunch dishes.

"Hello, Grandmother dear."

She almost dropped the plate back into the soapy water.

"Don't you ever knock, Drake?"

"I didn't want to be on the doorstep for too long."

She looked away, then dropped her hands into the suds to continue washing the dishes.

"I need to talk to you and Granddad."

"We heard about what's happening."

"How? The newspapers, or have you been talking to someone?"

She grabbed a cloth and wiped the sink area, and then after wringing the cloth out, she pulled the plug in the sink, turned, and looked at Drake.

"The police came by yesterday. They were looking for you and your parents, my daughter."

"They were looking for Mom and Dad, too?"

"Yes. Apparently, they're missing. The police think you were at their house on Hunter Street late the other night. Is that true?"

He stepped forward. "There's a lot to discuss. Can you get Grandpa, and we'll all talk about this at the same time?"

"Why are you here, Drake? You have to understand how hard this has been on us. Have you done what they say you have?"

He stared into her eyes momentarily and then said, "No."

She wiped her hands on her small apron that dangled from her waist. "Okay, I'll get your grandpa."

She stepped away and walked upstairs. Drake took a minute to check the front windows—no unusual activity. As far as he could tell, no one watched the place.

Footsteps approached from behind. He turned and looked into the eyes of his grandfather. The man balanced precariously on his cane.

"Aren't you supposed to be in a wheelchair?" Drake asked. "Here, let me help you."

Granddad held up a hand. "Wait," he said in his familiar deep voice. "Why are you here?"

Drake thought of squeaky doors in horror movies when his grandfather spoke. He always loved that voice.

"I have questions."

They stood in the living room, looking at each other. After a long pause, his grandfather spoke first.

"So do I. Shall we talk?"

Drake nodded. His grandfather walked awkwardly as he led Drake to the kitchen. After they were seated, his grandmother put the kettle on.

"You start," his grandfather said.

"Where were you born?" Drake asked.

"Here."

"Yeah, but where, specifically?"

Granddad shook his head. "One question each. Be more specific if you want better answers." He paused to cough into his inner elbow. Drake heard phlegm and wondered if smokers ever learned. He has been smoking since he was a teenager and now dying of emphysema, he still smokes a couple a day. Maybe that's where Drake's mother caught her cancer? Secondhand smoke when she was growing up.

"Where are your parents?" Granddad asked.

Drake leaned back in his seat as his grandmother approached with the hot kettle. She poured three teas and set a small tray with sugar, cream, and stir sticks on the table. Drake marveled at how formal they were. Where did they get it from? Another era? Or could it be an upbringing in another country?

"I have no idea. But I will tell you what I do know so we can get through this twenty-question thing faster."

His grandmother sat beside her husband of fifty-six years and clasped her hands together, only separating them to sip her tea while Drake started at the beginning. He told them everything from his dad giving him the address to picking up the medical weed to this morning seeing nothing in the news about last night's murder at the warehouse where he worked as a forklift operator.

"So that's why I'm here. These Hungarians continually say I'm family. I have no idea how that could be true as I was born here, my parents were, and you both claim to be." He paused and looked off to the side. "Could there be a connection all the way back to either one of your parents?"

During his sordid tale, his grandmother grew edgy. Granddad stayed as placid as a lump of ice.

She nudged him and whispered, "Tell him. Now's the time."

Granddad looked at her, a stern expression on his face. Drake thought he heard his grandfather's teeth gnashing together.

"It's never a good time," Granddad said.

"Tell me what?" Drake asked. "Seriously, if you know something, then now *is* the time. Your own kid's life is at stake here."

Granddad edged sideways in his seat and picked up his cane. He used it to get to his feet and then walk away.

"Hey, wait. People are trying to kill me. If you two know something."

His grandfather stopped and turned back. "If you must know, then she will tell you. I won't because I can't. This wasn't my fault. I did it to protect my family. I'd do it again. This is your fault, Drake. You started this in high school." He paused to cough again. Looking back at Drake, he said, "I'm sorry. I wish things were different. I'll be dead soon, and my secrets will die with me. Goodbye, Drake."

His grandfather walked away, leaving behind a stunned grandson. Drake felt the shock hit him like a physical weight.

His grandmother touched his arm.

Drake snapped his head around to face her. She leaned away at his sudden movement.

"I didn't mean to startle you," she said.

"Sorry, my nerves have been shot over the past few days. Can you tell me what Granddad was talking about?"

She nodded and lowered her head. Her hands came together on the table. She began picking at one of her nails.

"It all started when we were teenagers. We fell in love in

a war-torn country."

"What? Seriously? You two aren't from Canada?"

His grandmother looked up at him and then shook her head back and forth. A tear in her eye threatened to escape the lid.

"I was born in a hospital in Budapest. Your grandfather was born in a small town called Esztergom near the Slovakian border. In those days, it was called Czechoslovakia. We met when we were seventeen in a city called Pecs."

Drake held up his hands. "Wait. Does this mean there is a family connection? Monika isn't completely fucked?"

She nodded. "There's a connection."

"Then why are they going after me?"

"Let me explain. Sip your tea, and I will tell you." She poured more into her cup and set down the kettle. "We married in 1954 at the age of twenty. I was pregnant with your mother by the time I was twenty-two. That was a difficult year."

She took another sip of her tea. Drake's head spun.

"1956 was the year the Russians invaded Hungary—the Russian Revolution. Tanks drove up the main streets of Budapest. I was pregnant, and I didn't want to live in a war-torn country or attempt to raise our child there, so your grandfather swore to me that he would get us out. Thousands upon thousands of Hungarians left during that horrible time. But we didn't have proper papers. We were stuck."

"So what happened?" Drake asked.

"Your grandfather had a friend from when he was five years old. This man was important then. He called him. Papers were arranged. Within twenty-four hours, we were on

Canadian soil."

"Wow, that guy must've been somebody. How come no one knows? Why the secret?" Then he thought of something else. "How come you two don't have accents?"

"We were both well-educated in British English when we were in Hungary. After being in Canada for two years, we had the Canadian English down pat with virtually no accent. Do you know how long it took to learn the *th* sound in English? That was a tough one."

"Then why all the secrecy?" Drake asked.

"Your grandfather was moving up in the circles he ran in in Hungary. He staunchly believed in a little-known sect that was making ground in the political world. Let me be clear, though, he was no criminal. They stood for a free Hungary. A democratic one. To avoid persecution, we ran under assumed names and with an assumed identity with fake passports thanks to his friend."

"You've mentioned this friend twice. Should I know him?"

His grandmother looked down at her teacup and spoke without lifting her head. "His name is Ferenczi, Sandor. He is Monika's grandfather."

Drake didn't think he could be more stunned than he was. Nothing ever had shocked him like those two words. *Monika's grandfather*. He stood up to pace the kitchen floor.

"So what did those papers say?" he asked.

"Ferenczi had ties in Canadian immigration. He wrote it up that I was his sister. He sponsored us through their family reunification program so we would be fast-tracked. To this day, the records still show that Ferenczi is my brother, even though I only met the man twice, and he grew up in the same neighborhood as your grandfather."

"Oh, my shit. Are you *even* serious? I think I'm getting it. Monika thinks we're second cousins. And it's all—"

"We could never have guessed you would attend the same school." She cut him off. "It had been decades. When your mother said you were getting serious with a girl in high school, we naturally wanted to meet her. It all came together one Sunday at dinner who she was. Her accent gave her away. Your grandfather and I knew it instantly. After a little research, we saw that Monika led right back to Ferenczi. It's not a big deal, really, for two reasons. We aren't *actually* family, and relationships at that age rarely last. We thought you would break up within months. At worst, a year, and you'd be on to another girl."

While pacing, he tried to remember something Kory had said.

"That's why Kory said Monika had called him. It was set up. She wanted to break up with me and have me roughed up. She must've found the connection somehow and thought I knew about it, too. She blamed me for being in a relationship, according to her, *knowingly*, with a cousin, and it disgusted her. Especially because she really loved me." He turned and faced his grandmother. "We were going to elope."

"Oh my," she covered her mouth with her hand. "We had no idea."

"Yeah, great. Now my parents are missing, Attila and Mike are dead, and the police think I'm a rapist murderer. Those poor girls. What they must've gone through."

"But you aren't related to Monika. This isn't our fault. Monika did this. It wouldn't have mattered if you eloped. We were sworn to secrecy because we could've been deported if immigration ever found out our documents were fake. Going back to Hungary would've been a death sentence. So instead, we got to stay in the country where the fences are made of sausages."

"What? What did you say the fences are made of?"

"Sausages. It's something old Hungarians say, which means people are so rich over here that even the fences are made of food because there's an abundance."

"I need to talk to people. I have to talk to Monika. I need to call Spencer. This story has to be told." Drake continued to pace back and forth.

"Your grandfather would never let that happen. Without his friend Ferenczi, we wouldn't be here. We'd probably be dead. Your grandfather gave his word this story would never see the light of day."

Drake leaned in close and put his hands on the kitchen table. "But don't you see? People are dying because of that secrecy. People have been murdered. I may be killed before this is over."

"No." She shook her head. "We will call the police and tell them everything together. I will explain our side, and you can tell them what you told us. They will believe it. Once they pick up Laszlo and Monika, everything will be over."

"I disagree. Give me the papers that showed you as a family with Ferenczi. Where do you have them?"

He detected movement behind him. Drake spun around so fast that he almost bumped into his grandfather.

"Take it easy," his grandfather spit out. "You might give me a heart attack before the emphysema kills me."

His grandfather held up a hand. In it were a set of car keys.

"Take these. Use my old Malibu and drive to your parents' house. The document you're looking for is in their basement. From what I heard of your story, it sounds like they won't be home, nor will anyone else. Use the defective back door and get downstairs. Once you get through the laundry room, turn left. The room on the left has boxes of papers. You'll find what you need in there."

"What will I find?" Drake asked.

"Proof of our births," he pointed at his wife, "in two different parts of Hungary to two different parents." He coughed again. "You will also see the fabricated immigration documents. Everything you need is there."

"Once I get all that, what next?"

"After you leave, we will call this Spencer Milton you spoke of and give him the pictures of the police cruiser you photographed last night, and we'll tell him everything you said and everything we know. He will understand it as we do when I'm through with him."

For the first time in days, Drake felt a sense of hope creeping in. Things were coming together. Once Spencer was brought into the loop, getting this monkey off his back would be much easier. While Drake was busy grabbing the proof he needed for Monika's motive, Spencer could be at the loading docks and looking over the crime scene. Maybe everything would be okay after all.

Drake grabbed the keys, hugged his grandparents, and ran for the door. At the last second, he turned around and asked, "Why did you say I started it earlier?"

"What are the chances that you would find a girlfriend—and not just any girlfriend—but the one that just happens to be a direct relative of my best friend from when I was a kid?

The same guy we're supposed to be related to? Incredible odds. When you fell for Monika, it all started then."

"Yeah, but seriously, how was I to know? How could that be my fault?"

"I was assigning blame. I know what I did to get us out of Hungary. The secrets were supposed to die with us. When you fell for Monika, exposure seemed more real. I blamed you, and now I am fixing that. Take my car. Get your proof, and I will call the police on myself. There's no one to blame. We all do what we think is right at the time."

Drake thought about it for another few seconds.

"One more thing. Whatever happened to Ferenczi?"

"He died of a stroke about twelve years ago. It was a week after Monika went missing. Crazy timing." He paused and looked down. "Come to think of it, Monika's dad was pretty pissed at that time. He said he would get his revenge for whoever hurt his daughter. That was one of the reasons Laszlo joined the Toronto Police Force."

"Do you know where they live?" Drake asked.

"All I know is that they are all in Toronto, and Monika stayed in Hungary. It sounds like Monika is back in Canada seeking revenge for what happened that night, which, from how you told it, was her fault, anyway."

Drake grabbed the door handle and looked back. "Call Spencer Milton. Tell him everything. Explain that Monika is attempting to reenact that night twelve years ago by making me suffer as she did. Hurting Kory and Avery's girlfriends was her way of showing them how it feels to do that to someone. Blaming it on me will ruin my future, as hers was ruined by rape. Call him. Make him hear you. Make him understand. My life depends on it."

He stepped outside but held the door open.

"Granddad, you did extraordinary things to save your family members years ago. Do it again. Save me."

Drake ran out the door, jumped in the Malibu, and headed for the 401 Heroes Highway.

He got off the Don Valley Parkway within forty-five minutes and started for his parents' house.

Would the police have it staked out?

He decided to drive around the area a few times, looking for anyone sitting in a car on a stakeout, whatever that looked like. Drake wondered if he would recognize professionals on the job or not. No one would suspect the Malibu, so an extra drive around couldn't hurt.

After twenty minutes and seeing nothing untoward, he parked three houses down and sat, watching. No one approached his car. An old woman was out walking a small terrier, but that was it for this early afternoon on Hunter Street.

He opened the door, got out, and locked the vehicle behind him. The spot where he'd parked a few days ago was occupied by another vehicle. The police must have towed his old Pontiac.

Nonchalantly, as if he lived there, Drake walked up the walkway of his parents' home, followed the path to the back, and hopped onto the deck.

The anxiety he felt decreased. The police weren't watching the house. No one was here. The police knew his parents weren't home. They were missing just as he was. Resources of the Toronto Police Department wouldn't be that grand as to have permanent officers watching the house of a missing couple.

The sun beat down on the nape of his neck as he eased the back door open. A soft breeze cooled him as he pulled the vertical blinds aside and stepped into the kitchen.

What was he going to do with the documents anyway? Would Monika listen if he had proof? How would she feel once she had learned the truth? All this was her fault. All the people who had died horrible deaths were going to be on her conscience. She'd probably kill Drake, anyway. The information would be too hurtful. He would have to take it to Spencer first and let him deal with Monika.

He walked across the kitchen, grabbed the stairwell door, and paused there.

Doubt was a traitor. There was no way anyone was in the house, but the Hungarians always surprised him with how resourceful they were.

No reason not to be proactive.

He turned back and ran to the kitchen counter. A wooden block with eight steak knives sat on it. He lifted one out, turned the handle in his hand so the blade angled along the length of his arm, cutting edge aimed away from him, and walked back to the basement door.

The knob was cold. He twisted it slowly and eased the door open.

This must be how paranoia feels.

He hopped down three stairs, then turned on the landing to go down the last eight. Once in the laundry room, his anxiety spiked.

If humans have an internal radar, mine's pinging. But why? What am I missing?

He had encountered no one. There had been no sounds except for the ones he made, yet it was almost like he was being watched.

Or maybe it was the feeling of being trapped. Down in the basement of a house could be scary after the last two days of running.

Attila was dead now. Laszlo would be seeking revenge. There'd be no niceties the next time they met.

Laszlo had a gun.

Drake didn't.

He opened the last door that led into the main basement area and stepped inside. He hit the light switch.

Overhead pot lights illuminated the finished basement theater room. Drake turned left and entered the storage room, where he saw boxes of files piled atop each other against the wall.

He ran over, dropped the knife on the floor, and began lifting down box after box. After reading the box covers to determine what was in them, he stopped at the box that said, *Mom and Dad's Papers*.

That had to be it.

He flipped off the lid and grabbed the first file folder labeled with the date 1956.

It wasn't the anxiety that saved him. It wasn't his reflexes.

In the end, his grandparents' file folder cushioned the blow.

The file room was designed as a bedroom. A small closet sat three feet to his right. There was no door in the closet, as his parents always just used this room for storage.

He turned, arms up, the file folder still in his right hand. The blow was so vicious that both hands got hit in unison. The sound of his left wrist breaking was loud. The folder barely protected his right. He shouted out in pain as the weapon continued forward, connecting with his right temple.

The pain came in a rush, like a wave washing over him. The wave caused a darkness so complete that Drake welcomed it over the reality of being aware.

He was out before he hit the floor.

Chapter 14

OFTEN, ONE CAN DISCERN the exact moment they wake up. The dream that is so suddenly shattered by the drill of the alarm clock or the moment consciousness arrives at the sound of a morning bird singing outside the open window.

For Drake, a searing pain woke him from his slumber. The kind of pain he had never felt before.

"Wake up!" a woman yelled.

He moaned, rolled his head, and tried to open his eyes. His wounded wrist protested the movement. His moan grew to a wail as he wished he could go back under.

"Wake up!"

He got his eyes open to slits. "What …?"

"No, this is my time. Your part is over."

"What are you talking about—"

"No! You have done enough."

The pain was intense. He heard her, but focusing on her

words became a chore.

She slapped him violently, his face snapping to the side.

"That was for my brothers." Emotion choked her voice.

He was still in the basement of his parents' house. He was sitting in a wooden chair, his arms tied behind him, his legs secure. A single rope was wrapped around his chest, securing him to the chair and arresting all movement.

"What are you doing?" he asked.

She stepped in front of his chair and looked down at him. "This was supposed to be easy."

He met her gaze. "Easy, how?" The pain in his wrist numbed, although any kind of movement spiked it. He wondered how bad the break was and how long before the bones would start to fuse in the wrong position.

"After killing Anne." Monika waved a finger at him like they were in grade school. "You were supposed to be caught in her apartment, but somehow, you escaped from that building on Victoria Park. Then we placed Michelle in your bedroom. I thought that would do it. But no, you got away again. My brother fired his weapon to scare you and to get the police called to the area so they would find the body. But still, you resourceful pig, you remained a free man."

"But I didn't do anything."

Monika slapped him again. Pain shot through his arm. He couldn't help the squeal that escaped his lips. She walked over to the small basement window and peeked through the blinds.

"Now I have lost my brothers because of you. I should've just killed you from the start. But in my urge to protect you from my brothers, I made them swear not to kill you."

"What has happened to me isn't protection. It's disgusting what you've done. And haven't you heard that one about digging two graves and revenge and shit? Well, you better start digging."

She turned back to him and sauntered over like she didn't have a care in the world. "I protected you from my father all those years ago. After they found me near death at the bottom of that cliff, they rounded up some men and went hunting for you. I begged them not to. I explained that we had both fallen down. You got knocked out and were in the hospital. I fell to the bottom of the cliff. The evidence of rape from Kory and Avery was explained as what teenagers do. I said we were having too much fun and I fell. I begged them to drop the issue. After a while, they believed things had just gotten out of hand. I begged them to take me back to Hungary so I could live there."

"So why now?" Drake asked. "Why do all this?"

"Because I'm dying." She sat in a wooden chair opposite him. "If they ever caught me for all that I have done in the last few days and I had to go to court on charges of murder, it wouldn't matter. I'd be dead before I ever saw a jail cell. Kory gave me Hepatitis C, and you know us Hungarians, we love to drink. By just living my life, I accelerated the disease. I have a rare blood type and cannot find a liver. I will be dead soon, and it all stems back to that night when you and I went to the lake."

Drake stared into her eyes. "*You* called Kory that night. You set it up that way. This, in no way, was my fault."

"I disagree. Your grandmother is my grandfather's sister. We are second cousins, and you know that."

"I know it now because they just told me. But what they

also told me was that it was a lie to get them into Canada during the Russian Revolution in Hungary. An immigration ploy."

"What would you know of revolutions in Hungary? When I asked my grandfather, he said the relationship connection was true. He wouldn't lie to me. After that, he set up a meeting with your grandparents, and they said in front of me when I was only eighteen years old that they were brother and sister. I told them that I would stop dating you after that."

"You have an odd way of breaking up with people. And, of course, they would all say it was true. They had a lie to maintain. Their secret was more important than a boyfriend, girlfriend thing."

"Drake, I knew you knew already. It was gross to think we would marry each other, yet we were related. You had to be taught a lesson because you lied by omitting that information. If I didn't ask Kory to come and pretend to rough you up, my father said he would break both your legs. Again, I protected you. I begged him to let me handle it. You would be dead and buried by now if it wasn't for me. You're such an ungrateful pig for what I've done for you, sacrificed for you." She leaned closer. "I loved you!"

He couldn't wrap his head around her logic. Her story got more and more twisted as she told it. Did all this happen because she was *protecting* him? Because she *loved* him?

"I came here," Drake said, "because my grandfather told me the truth was in the file I held when you broke my wrist. He was born in Esztergom, and my grandmother was born in Budapest. They met in a city called Pecs. They asked your grandfather to lie about the family status to get them into

Canada unhindered. They aren't *family*. It was a lie. You and I could've been together. This was all for naught."

Monika shook her head back and forth. "I can't believe you. Even now, you try to sully my grandfather's memory. Like he would lie to me. You are pathetic. You sit there and try to weasel your way out of this like it was all my doing, all my fault. You will die for this. You will suffer like I did."

He hoped the police or Spencer Milton had talked to his grandparents and were on their way. Or maybe the cops were outside listening in at that moment. At the very least, Drake hoped Spencer had asked his officers to be looking for the old Malibu he had driven there. Drake had been lucky—very lucky. Maybe it wasn't over yet. Stalling whatever she had planned was the only way to wait for an opening or to allow Spencer time to do his job and stop Monika.

"When you said you lost your brothers, what did you mean?" Drake asked.

"At your warehouse, Attila was shot and killed. After you escaped last night, we stayed behind to remove both bodies and clean up the sand you threw in Laszlo's eyes. I was there. I was waiting in the other room for you. And now Laszlo is on the run because we found out that Spencer Milton was looking for Laszlo ten minutes before you got here. To keep the cops away from this place so I can finish with you, my brother called Spencer and told him where your parents are hiding out. My brother said he had you with him and that both of you were on your way to meet your parents."

His hope died. No one was coming. "But when Spencer goes to where Laszlo is, and I'm not there, what then? And what were you doing at the warehouse last night? I didn't see you. Why were you waiting for me?"

Monika pulled out a syringe from her purse. "I wanted to give you this."

Shit! "What's that?"

"My blood. It contains the Hepatitis C virus."

"You're not serious." His stomach dropped so far it felt like it hit the chair. The urge to vomit rose in his throat.

"I am deadly serious. After all the shit that went down, I plan to have everyone go through what happened to me. Kory and Avery's girlfriends were raped, beaten, and left for dead like they did to me. You get blamed for it, so your life is ruined as mine was. Kory and Avery die for their crimes, and you will now get the injection. In fifteen years or so, you will have physical difficulties like I have, and eventually, you will die too, after suffering as I have." She paused, looked down at the needle, and then back at Drake. "Unless, of course, you die from the fall."

"The fall? What fall?" He squirmed in his chair.

She smiled down at him. In that smile and behind those eyes, he saw her insanity.

"No. You're not going to ..." he whispered.

Monika nodded. "Yes. You get the same fate I was dealt."

"But why? *You* had Kory come out that night. Things got out of hand. Now, all the people responsible are dead. It wasn't my fault."

His pleadings fell on deaf ears. Spencer wasn't going to save him. No one could now. His wrist was surely broken. He couldn't defend himself with a broken wrist. The ropes that held him were seriously tight. He figured it had more to do with keeping the veins in his arms bulging for the needle than simply securing him.

"You're not suffering enough yet," Monika said as she

walked to the window again.

"You expecting someone?" Drake asked.

"I will not allow anyone to stop me. If any cops show up here within the next hour, I will kill them all. I'm beyond caring." She turned back to Drake. "Tell me something first."

He turned his head around slowly. "What?"

"Did you really love me? I mean, back in high school?"

"Of course I did. I wanted to marry you. Since that time, my life has never been the same. I tried to date once or twice, but nothing came of it."

She strode back to him and sat down. "Did you know we were related back then?"

"Absolutely not," Drake said without hesitation.

"You see, that's why you have to suffer."

Drake shook his head. His wrist flared. "What? That doesn't make any sense."

Her head twitched. He saw it. There was a subtle movement as she lowered her gaze to his knees.

What's wrong with her?

"Even now, with all that has happened, you still lie to me. You're just that kind of person, I guess."

There was no use. Hope was a bird flitting around his head, unsure where to land. It became an irritant, and with her words, the bird called Hope flew out the window.

She moved to his side. The needle in her hand was filled with what looked like blood. This had to be a joke. There was no way anyone could be so cruel. He needed to stall her.

"Tell me one thing," he said.

"What?"

"Who sent the cards?" Drake asked.

"Oh, those." Monika laughed. "That was my father's

idea. He said it had something to do with the old ways of fear. Something about marking the dead before they're killed. He's the one who managed that. Everything else was my plan. My brothers got to handle lots of the details, and they both got a bonus rape out of it—sex, you know, what all men want, what all men *need,* but with the added bonus of control over their victim. As far as I know, they spent over ten hours taking turns on Avery's girlfriend before they asphyxiated her. Free sex and murder because the police are one hundred percent sure it was you."

Drops of liquid flew past his face and hit his leg. He looked up at her. She had nudged the plunger on the syringe a notch.

"Wouldn't want to inject any air into you. The last thing I want is for you to die that way. Too fast, too quick. Not enough suffering."

She grabbed his arm with her free hand.

His heart rate spiked. "Wait!"

She paused. "What? You won't be able to stop me."

"Just wait. Isn't there something we could do? It doesn't have to end this way."

"Yes, it does. There's nothing left to say."

"But there is. Before you do that thing … maybe, could you …" he stammered over his tongue. "Could you at least read the file I held when you hit me with that club or whatever the fuck it was?"

She let go of his arm and walked around to face him. "I read it when you were knocked out. All it said was that your grandmother was the sister of my grandfather, who, by the way, died a week or so after I fell from the cliff. I still think the events of that week pushed him over. So there's another dead body to add to your collection."

"Monika, this isn't right. Look at the other files in the box. There's supposed to be one that states the opposite. Our grandparents aren't related. They never were. You gotta look."

His face felt hot and flushed. He breathed out rapidly, panting to the point of near hyperventilation. Would this nightmare ever end? What would happen to him after the injection?

Monika checked the window again. In the corner by a small cabinet sat a baseball bat. He hadn't noticed it before. That must've been the weapon she'd hit him with.

His vision started to blur. He wondered how close he was to passing out.

Monika turned back around. "There's nothing left to discuss. It's been fun chatting. You know, catching up. But now, we must continue."

"Monika, this isn't rational—it isn't right. You can't do this. Please, I beg you."

He pulled on his restraints. There was no budge at all. The pain seemed dulled by his heightened state of shock. He was locked down in the chair. Stars entered his vision.

A smug look crossed her face as she held the needle. Then she stared at it like it was crystal meth, and she was a user ready for the next hit.

"Here we go." She giggled. In her eyes, he saw insanity again. Monika was completely gone.

"No!" Drake yelled. "Wait. Just tell me one more thing. Why are you doing this? I mean, I know you got a raw deal, but why me? You loved me once. What did I ever do to you?"

She grabbed his arm, slapped the inside of his elbow

several times, and looked up at him.

"You were my boyfriend. You were supposed to protect me. None of this would've happened if you had been more of a man."

"That's crazy. How could I protect you? Avery had knocked me out. I was gone. And besides, *you* set it up. You need to take some responsibility for this."

"I do. I own it. All of it. And that's why everyone involved is dead or will be dead soon. Sorry, Drake, but you fucked up."

"You are so wrong. Listen, Monika, don't. Think about it."

She looked at the roof of the basement. After two seconds, she looked back at him and said, "Okay, thought about it. Nothing changes."

He struggled under the grip of his restraints. Surprisingly, even though there wasn't any give, the weight of his head and the motion he started caused the chair to tilt and fall to the side, away from her.

"That doesn't matter, Drake. I can do it easier from there."

He saw her place the needle against the inside of his right arm. He was about to utter another plea, but the needle's tip broke his skin.

His eyes widened. It felt like his heart stopped.

Monika, with a wild and crazy look on her face, depressed the plunger into Drake's arm, forcing her Hepatitis C-infected blood into his veins.

He screamed.

His eyes watered. It was like he could feel it course through him. He felt diseased. He felt ruined. It wasn't fair.

He'd done nothing wrong. Why was this happening?

She stood and walked out of his vision.

He thrashed and screamed again. His face felt red with anger, his forehead covered in sweat.

When he looked at his arm, a droplet of blood trickled down from the tiny hole where her blood had entered. The tiny hole through which he had just been murdered.

Her feet entered his vision. Beside them was the tip of the baseball bat.

"Shut up!" she yelled and raised the bat's end.

It came down hard on the top of Drake's head.

Then, nothing mattered anymore.

Chapter 15

DRAKE WONDERED WHICH HURT more, his head or his wrist. He tried to move in the confined trunk space and decided his wrist won the pain contest. Both arms had been tied behind him for so long since the bone broke that he hadn't been able to assess how bad it looked.

He moved his right hand slowly and touched the flesh of his left. A large bump had formed around his wrist—the swelling was severe.

The car hit a bump of some kind. His head smacked the underside of the trunk lid in the area where the bat had made contact with his skull. *A migraine would be more pleasant*, he thought as he gritted his teeth and waited for the pain to subside.

The engine slowed, and then he heard gravel under the tires.

The whole time he lay awake, he knew this had to be a

nightmare. No way would another human being do what Monika had done. How could she inject her contaminated blood into him? He reeled at the thought. How could human beings be so cruel?

The car slowed and then stopped. He heard her open the car door and felt the vibration as it was slammed shut.

The heat in the trunk had been bearable, but now it seemed to increase with every second of waiting.

The trunk key slid into the lock. There was a click, and then light filled the space. The setting sun was almost touching Lake Ontario in the west. He adjusted his eyes to the light, blinking rapidly.

Monika stood in front of the trunk. The area of the parking lot that he could see was empty. As his eyes adjusted, he looked into Monika's face and couldn't recognize the woman he once knew. She had scars that were far worse than her jaundiced skin. She looked sick, and her eyes offered a sense of sociopath.

"What now?" he asked, his own voice foreign to him.

Her right arm moved behind her, and she produced a knife.

"Whoa ..."

Monika bent into the trunk and reached around him to cut the restraints that bound his wrists.

His arms were free.

This was the first time he had seen his left wrist, and it turned his stomach.

"Look what you did," he said. "I need a doctor."

"No." Monika shook her head. "You need a coroner. Get out of the trunk, or I'll shoot you where you lay."

The knife had disappeared. A gun was in her hand.

"If you're going to kill me anyway, just shoot me. Get it over with."

She lowered the weapon until the barrel rested on his forehead. "Don't be stupid, Drake. Get out of the trunk."

The cold steel of Monika's weapon had a frightening feel to it. After a moment, the weapon eased off his skin. He used his right hand to turn and get his feet under him. After almost slipping and falling once, he managed to exit the trunk without hurting his wounded wrist further.

"Walk," Monika commanded.

The baseball bat lay on the gravel by the car's back tire. She was a woman of many weapons. A knife, a bat, and a gun. What was she expecting? A rumble with the Outsiders?

He started walking toward the cliff. This was not the time to be stupid. He didn't pretend to know why they were there. It started here in this parking area twelve years ago, and Monika intended it to end here.

She was going to push Drake over the hundred-foot drop to the rocks and water below and allow fate to decide if he was to live or not, as it was decided for Monika.

Ten feet from the edge, Drake felt a certain kind of peace. He was dead anyway now that Hepatitis C raged through his veins. Monika had killed him already. Now, she only offered him a faster way out.

How could he ever clear his name with the police? It would take years. They always assumed you were guilty before the courts had a chance to examine the case. The media would hound his parents. His grandparents might have immigration issues if everything became public knowledge. His boss, Mike, was dead, so there was no job to return to. He was sure his landlord wouldn't welcome him back anytime soon. She had already killed him. This was just a formality now.

Yet, even through all that, he'd take it if he saw an opening. Self-preservation was a severe force. But a stronger motivation was to rid the world of people like Monika. Hearing what Kory and Avery had done with their lives was beyond this horror. Having killed Kory with his own hands had felt good. Not in a sick sense, he assured himself. In a good sense. Some people should die. The world was a better place for it.

If he got the chance, Monika would have to die as well.

Three feet from the edge. He stopped and looked down. There wasn't a good place to aim. Rocks jutted left and right. Water sloshed in around them with each wave. The sun lowered farther, and the light of dusk was just enough to see that his chances of survival were slim.

"Move to the side about ten feet," she ordered.

He looked at her. The gun was held low by her side.

"Then what?" he asked.

"Just move along the edge ten more feet. Get closer to those bushes and that tree."

"You really want to reenact it exactly the way it happened?"

"Yes. Now move."

Drake walked, his arms swinging freely, the left wrist numb.

He walked through the area where they had parked that fateful night. Then his feet stepped over the space where Monika had been raped.

When he got to the bushes, he stepped around them and stopped a couple of feet from the edge.

"Monika, can I say one last thing?"

"Make it good. You go over in seconds."

"I'm sorry."

Her gaze faltered for a brief moment. The gun twitched in her hand.

"I'm sorry," he repeated. "For what they did to you. I'm sorry we didn't marry, and I'm sorry for the children we didn't have. After you turned up in Hungary and the police stopped harassing me about you being a missing person, my life never went back to normal. I missed you dearly. I loved you. A part of me still remembers the young, sweet Monika. That part still loves you. So, I'm sorry." He waited a moment, then added, "Goodbye, Monika."

It broke her composure. Drake remembered reading somewhere many years ago that even in the worst human beings, there's a little goodness somewhere.

A tear edged down her cheek. She wiped it with her free hand in a rapid gesture and motioned for him to get down.

"Lie on the ground. You will roll over just like I did. If you live, your debt to me has been paid. You will never see me or any member of my family again."

"Monika, we don't have to do this."

"Lie down, Drake, or I will shoot you in each leg to make sure you hit the ground, and then your chances of survival will be greatly reduced when you hit the bottom."

He took one last look around. Not a car in sight. No one had shown up to save him. It was over. He had nothing left up his sleeve. No tricks, no words. Even if he tried to overpower her, she held a gun, a knife in a sheath somewhere behind her, and he had a broken wrist.

He turned and looked over the edge at this new spot. It

wasn't any better than the other spot. He had no idea how Monika survived the fall that fateful night.

The sun continued its descent.

Drake started his. He lowered himself to one knee and then the other. Monika stood over him and watched, her attention riveted on what he was doing. Then, slowly, he eased down and lay on his right side. Two full rolls, and he would be gone.

"Goodbye, Drake."

She lifted her foot and pushed. He rolled onto his back. As he started to roll onto his left, he remembered his wrist. The pain would be intense. He resisted her prodding.

"I'm sorry, Drake, but this is how it has to be."

He could roll onto his back again and look up at her. The gun had come into his vision. She was aiming it at his left arm.

"This will help. It's the only way."

She fired her weapon. His arm shook like it had been punched. Horrified, Drake raised his arm to look. A red hole had formed in the center of his forearm. Blood began trickling from the hole.

She shot me, for fuck's sake.

Her foot attempted to roll him again. He resisted. There was no way he was going to lean on his broken wrist and now shot arm.

Grinding his teeth, shouting, and using his right hand for support, Drake fought her until he was on his back again.

"I can't believe you shot me!" he yelled.

"Enough of this," she stammered.

Standing over him, Monika raised her gun and aimed it at his face. "You had your chance to fall. Now you die."

The weapon was two feet away. After her perfect aim into his forearm, he was sure she wouldn't miss.

As her finger squeezed the trigger, Drake screamed.

The gun went off.

Chapter 16

Drake opened his eyes. His heart raced as he tried not to hyperventilate.

Monika was no longer standing over him. He scanned his body for bullet wounds and found none. He leaned up on his good elbow and took in the scene.

Monika was hunkered down behind a tree trunk near the bushes. Blood oozed down the arm that had held her gun. The gun was in her left hand now.

Someone had shot her. But who?

He looked across to the other side of the parking lot, where a wall of trees seemed to be moving. His eyes focused, and then he understood what he was seeing. Over a dozen policemen in Emergency Task Force gear were hunkered behind the trees. One of them lifted a device in his hand and shouted for Monika to come out with her hands up.

"It's over," the ETF guy said. "Come out and leave your

weapon on the ground."

Drake didn't have time to wait. He was bleeding out, and at any moment, Monika could still shoot him. He got to his feet and stumbled away from her. Where he found the strength to get up and walk was a mystery as he continued to lose blood.

After making it about six feet, he looked back and saw her watching him. He wondered why she hadn't shot him, and then it occurred to him that she would only have a certain amount of bullets, and she would probably need them to get out of this alive.

"Drake Bellamy," the bullhorn roared. "Get down and stay down. Medics are on their way."

He took another step and then another. He walked into the open parking lot, standing between Monika and the authorities. There was one thing left for him to do. He had no choice. She had shot him. She had injected him with her virus. He was a walking dead man. He needed to finish this.

When he got to the side of the Malibu, he grabbed the baseball bat.

It was time to rid the world of another rapist. Monika had orchestrated the rapes and deaths of two women that were innocent of this carnage. She had taken everything from Drake. His ability to live a normal life. His integrity and his honor. Because of what she had done, Drake had been forced to kill a man.

And now he was going to stop her.

The loudspeaker behind him was shouting something about putting the bat down. He detected movement behind him.

Monika peeked around the edge of the tree and lifted her

weapon. It was her left hand. Her aim would suffer because of it.

She said something unintelligible.

His head felt light. The blood loss. The shock of being shot. Whatever it was, he was weakening quickly.

He made three fast strides and lifted the bat high in his right hand.

Monika fired at him from about five feet away. She fired again and again until the gun only clicked.

He felt two punches on his left leg. He jolted, swayed, paused momentarily, and then continued walking with a limp. The pain would come later. He didn't have a death wish, but did it really matter anymore? He stumbled again but stayed erect on the strength of his right leg.

One quick hop, and he was close enough to strike her.

The bullhorn screamed behind him.

Monika lowered her empty gun and smiled at him. She had resigned herself to her fate. Because of their relationship, this had all come about. It was Drake's fault. She would blame him and thus welcome him the killing blow. She was dead anyway. Why not make it quick?

He didn't care fuck all what she thought. After all she had done, this would feel good, righteous.

Men were running up behind him, yelling something.

He swung the bat one-handed.

Just before it connected with the side of her head, Monika blew him a kiss.

Then she crumpled at his feet, blood pouring out of the wound to her head.

He fell to his knees. Pain seared up his left leg like it was suddenly on fire. He looked down, sure he'd see flames.

Then he rolled onto the side with the unhurt arm and wrist.

Cops surrounded him. They pulled Monika away and secured her weapon.

He was eased around to lie on his back.

Spencer Milton removed his helmet and stood over Drake, shaking his head.

"You are one serious motherfucker. Why did you do that?"

Drake closed his eyes and slept the pain away.

Chapter 17

HE JUST WANTED TO keep sleeping. It was quiet and safe there. He wasn't being hunted or shot at. No one could touch him. But consciousness won out.

Drake rose from his pain-filled dreams into a pain-filled reality. His throat felt like he'd swallowed sandpaper. The hospital bed was inclined slightly. He leaned up and saw his mother reading a magazine in a chair near the corner.

He tried to speak, but his voice failed to work. A grunt escaped his lips instead.

His mother looked up from her reading. She threw the magazine aside and jumped from her chair.

"Oh, Drake, you're awake."

He lowered his head and waited until she came into his peripheral vision. After a moment, he looked up into her eyes. She was crying.

"It's been over eighteen hours since they brought you in.

You had surgery. Two bullets grazed your left leg. It'll heal well. They had to set your broken wrist, fix the bullet hole in your arm, and place it in a cast. Other than the cast on your left arm and wrist, all the bandages will be removed within a week or two. Everything will be fine now."

He wondered why she gave him the rundown the second he woke. Wasn't that a doctor's job? She'd spent a lot of time in hospitals recently with her cancer. Maybe that's how she wanted it: straight up. He saw that she wasn't being completely truthful with him, though.

He tried to ask *what was wrong*, but his voice was too scratchy.

She leaned over and came back into view with a glass of water and a bendable straw.

Reflex caused him to attempt to raise his right arm and grasp the cup, but something was tied to it. He looked down and saw an IV in his forearm. His left was covered in a huge cast.

The straw was placed softly in his mouth as his mother held the glass. He took cautious sips, swallowing slowly. The last thing he wanted was to get it into the wrong tube and have a coughing fit with so many broken and fucked up body parts.

"Easy," she said.

Can't she see that's what I'm doing?

The straw left his lips. He lowered his head, emptied his mouth, and tried to speak again.

"Wha ... is wrong?"

She looked down at him. "Well, nothing's wrong now, Drake. It's all over. They picked up Leslie and found the bodies he was planning to hide. It doesn't look like Monika will make it. She's out of surgery, but her prognosis isn't good. You hit her pretty hard. But it's not her head that's killing her."

"Surgery? Monika? Who Leslie?" he managed, his voice doing better, his throat lubricated.

"She had a fractured skull or something. Her liver is failing pretty badly. It doesn't look good for her. I can't believe she came back after all these years. And for what? To kill people? I'm so happy you two never got married."

"Who Leslie?"

"His Hungarian name is Laszlo. He was a cop. They picked him up at the American border on the Peace Bridge, trying to sneak across. They found two bodies dumped on a concession road north of Hamilton, where he said he'd stashed them. He's been arrested for everything. The picture you sent to Spencer confirmed the Hungarians' presence at Avery's apartment, and the picture of the cruiser outside your warehouse that your grandparents gave Spencer confirmed their presence there, too. After everyone was looking for a bald guy at the hospital and then Kory was found dead," she paused and shook her head back and forth while staring at the ground. "Leslie will spend a long time in jail for his crimes. But now, no one can locate their father. He's disappeared. They want to talk to him about all this, but he's vanished."

Drake had a dozen more questions racing through his mind. Weakness and fatigue overcame him, but he needed to know more before he slept.

"Where have you and Dad been for the last few days?"

"We were driven to a hotel on Plains Road in Burlington and kept prisoner until yesterday. These were the same guys who ordered your father to call you and send you to that apartment in Scarborough to purchase medical weed. Your father said he wouldn't do it, but they had guns. Some beast of a man stood guard with another animal rotating on twelve-hour shifts. We ate great and slept little. Yesterday afternoon, they stepped out and disappeared. Your father and I got in our car and drove home. It was that simple."

"Tell me, do you know … how Spencer came to be at the cliff by the lake?"

"He said he talked to your grandfather. Something about Monika wanting to recreate the past. Spencer had researched you and knew about the intense questioning you had undergone in high school regarding her missing persons case. It was still in the police records. So he knew the exact location. He sent men to our place on Hunter Street while he assembled a team of ETF agents to meet him at the cliff to wait. He was pretty sure Monika would show."

"Was he there the whole time?"

"He said he saw Monika pull up in Granddad's Malibu, but they didn't approach until he saw you."

"He waited too long. She could've pushed me off the cliff."

"I wasn't there, but he assured me you were safe the whole time. When she drew her weapon, Spencer said his men converged."

"Yeah, they came to the rescue, all right. I got shot, Mom. I could've died out there."

She looked away, her face a mask of concern. He could tell she was holding something back. He could see it in her eyes.

"What are you not telling me?"

She turned to him and started crying. Then she did

something that surprised him. She leaned over and hugged him while she sobbed.

"I'm so sorry, Drake. I'm so sorry."

"For what?" he asked. Maybe she was referring to everything that had happened. All of it and the trauma he'd gone through. Maybe seeing her son in a hospital bed having been shot does that to a mother because she wasn't the huggy type.

After a moment, she grabbed a Kleenex to dab at her eyes.

"Sorry for what?" he repeated.

"Spencer Milton has the whole story. He talked to your grandparents. He talked with us. He knows what Monika did and was attempting to do to you."

"Then why are you sorry?"

"Because they found a syringe in the basement of my house. There's a needle mark on your arm."

Drake lowered his head deeper into the pillow. For a moment, he'd forgotten that she'd injected him with Hep C.

The world became a dark shadow again.

"Monika injected me with that needle before she took me out to the cliff by Lake Ontario."

"That's what we figured when you were sleeping. Spencer brought the needle in to have it analyzed. They determined it was Monika's blood. They also found trace elements of the virus Hepatitis C in it."

He closed his eyes and tried to sleep. His mother was talking and crying again. She said something about the doctor testing his blood. The results would be back soon.

He turned his head away and drifted off to sleep, listening to his mother's voice like when he was five years old.

Chapter 18

WHEN HE WOKE AGAIN, both his parents were there. What woke him wasn't the pain as much as the talking. A small throb came from his leg. His wrist was still numb.

A doctor stood in a long white lab coat, talking to his parents.

"If it concerns me, start at the beginning," he interrupted.

His throat felt better, and he felt more rested. Home wouldn't be too far away now.

The doctor turned to him and smiled. "Glad you could join us, Drake. I have the results back from your blood work." The doctor smiled again, even wider if that were possible. "You do *not* have Hepatitis C."

Drake's chest deflated as he breathed out. He took a deep breath in again and said, "What? How's that possible? There were traces found in the blood in the needle. Monika said it was her blood. My mother told me the blood in the syringe was tested."

The doctor nodded. "It was her blood. I had it examined myself." He stepped away from Drake's parents and walked up to the bed to stand beside Drake. "The Hepatitis C virus can live outside the host body for up to four days. However, many experts think it usually survives only up to sixteen hours at room temperature. The virus Monika injected in you was already dead when it hit your bloodstream. She waited too long. You're in the clear. The wait time for results is usually about five days, but I had them check your blood in three. I will need you to come back in a few months for another test just to be sure, but I'm pretty confident you aren't in danger."

Once the doctor said sixteen hours, something Monika had said came back to him.

"You're right, Doctor. I don't have it, and I won't get it. Monika told me she was waiting for me at the docks where I work to give me the injection. It took her over twenty hours to catch up to me at your house." He nodded at his parents. "The virus must've died in that time. Oh shit, that's lucky."

He leaned back on the pillow and stared at the tiled ceiling.

He had walked right up to Monika with the baseball bat while she emptied her gun at him, thinking he was dead anyway. Lucky for him, she was such a poor shot.

Now, he wasn't going to die. At least not prematurely.

He had murdered Kory, and no one knew. The bald guy was being blamed for all of it. The bald Hungarian guy—Laszlo.

They had tried to frame him for everything, and in the end, Attila was dead, Laszlo was going to prison for life, and

Monika was dying while he walked out of the hospital a free man and completely healed soon enough.

It was truly over. He was safe. A normal life was his to have again.

The doctor stepped away, still smiling, and his mother walked up to the side of the bed. "While you've been recovering here in the hospital, our mail piled up at the house."

Why would his mother tell him about her mail? He hadn't lived with them for over ten years.

"There was a piece in there for you. Maybe it's a get-well card. I'll get it."

She walked to the table in the corner of the room. Numerous flower arrangements sat by the window. He hadn't noticed them before. Everything seemed so much more cheerful now that he was granted a reprieve in life.

He looked back at the ceiling, and then his mother came into view.

"Here it is."

She handed him a white envelope with his parents' address written on the outside. There was no return address.

"You don't know who sent it?" he asked.

"No, it's your mail. I didn't open it."

He tore the corner and used his index finger to slide along the top of the envelope, opening it as he went.

The card had a single rose on the front.

How nice.

He opened the card and read the inside.

He wasn't safe after all. This had only been the beginning. It was all starting up again.

But it couldn't. Why did it have to? Why him?

Monika's father had sent the note. The man whom the police were still looking for. It was the same kind of note that Avery and Kory had received.

He reread the inside of the card.

You have killed my son. You have killed my daughter. My other son will never see the light of day.

You have disgraced and defiled my family.

The same fate awaits you and your family.

I'm on my way.

You will not know when to expect me.

I'll see you soon.

About Jonas Saul

Jonas Saul is the bestselling author of the Sarah Roberts Series—more than two million sold!—and has written and published over sixty thrillers. After acquiring an agent, he signed several deals in Los Angeles, with MadRiver Pictures optioning his Sarah Roberts Series—over forty books!—(currently in development).

Jonas has often outranked Stephen King and Dean

Koontz on Amazon over the past decade. He's regularly invited to be a guest speaker, teacher, or workshop presenter at international writing conferences and film festivals worldwide. He hosts an annual writer's retreat in Greece, where he currently lives. He focuses his teaching on how to get tension and emotion in every scene, on every page, how he made it as a creator/writer, the path to success in this business, and the pitfalls to avoid. He also hosts a reading retreat in Greece with guest authors, yoga retreats, and hiking retreats. Visit the Imagine Greece Retreats website at www.imaginegreeceretreats.com, or email him directly to discuss an opportunity to join one of the retreats at jonas@imaginegreeceretreats.com.

Jonas is also a professional freelance editor. He works for several publishers and does private editing for clients, with many testimonials on his website at www.imaginepress.org, which details each author's response to Jonas's editing skills. Email Jonas directly for an editing quote at editor@imaginepress.org.

To book Jonas for a speaking engagement at a writer's conference/festival, to have him on your jury at a film festival, or even to say hello, email Jonas directly at jonassaul@icloud.com.

For updates on releases, hit the "Follow" button on Amazon or Bookbub, and join Jonas on Facebook, where he's most active.

Contact Jonas Saul

Linktree: Find me here

Email: jonassaul@icloud.com